ELVINA'S MIRROR

ELVINA'S MIRROR

Sylvie Weil

2009 • 5769
Philadelphia

Copyright © 2009 by Sylvie Weil
Originally published 2003 by L'école des loisirs
Translated from the French by Sylvie Weil

The Jewish Publication Society
2100 Arch Street, 2nd floor
Philadelphia, PA 19103
www.jewishpub.org

Design and composition by Claudia Cappelli
Cover illustration and design by Avi Katz

Manufactured in the United States of America

09 10 11 12 10 9 8 7 6 5 4 3 2 1

Library of Congress Cataloging-in-Publication Data:
Weil, Sylvie.
Elvina's mirror / Sylvie Weil. —1st ed.
p. cm.
Summary: In 1097 Troyes, France, fourteen-year-old Elvina reaches out to a shunned family of German Jews, eventually drawing her grandfather, Bible and Talmud scholar Solomon ben Isaac, into helping her new friend's cousin Ephraim, whose memories of the Crusaders' cruelty have driven him mad.
ISBN 978-0-8276-0885-6 (alk. paper)
1. Jews—France—History—11th century—Juvenile fiction. 2. Crusades—First, 1096-1099—Juvenile fiction. [1. Jews—France—-History—11th century—Fiction. 2. Crusades—First, 1096-1099--Fiction. 3. Jews--Persecutions--Fiction. 4. Sex role—Fiction. 5. Rashi, 1040-1105—Fiction. 6. Troyes (France)—History—11th century—Fiction. 7. France—History—11th century--Fiction.] I. Title.
PZ7.W4333Elv 2009
[Fic]—dc22

2008030216

JPS books are available at discounts for bulk purchases for reading groups, special sales, and fundraising purchases. Custom editions, including personalized covers, can be created in larger quantities for special needs. For more information, please contact us at marketing@jewishpub.org or at this address: 2100 Arch Street, Philadelphia, PA 19103.

For Eric

The Elvina Trilogy

In French
Le mazal d'Elvina
Le miroir d'Elvina
Elvina et la fille du roi Salomon

———✦———

In English
My Guardian Angel
Elvina's Mirror

SUMMARY OF *MY GUARDIAN ANGEL*

(Scholastic Paperbacks, 2007)

Part I of the Elvina Trilogy

It is the early spring of the year 1096. Just as the holiday of Purim is approaching, thousands of Crusaders on their way to Jerusalem have set up camp in the countryside around Troyes, in Champagne. They have been known to kill Jews and burn their houses. The Jewish community is worried; ordinary life is disrupted.

Elvina, who is almost thirteen, carries on an imaginary dialogue with her mazal. All human beings, her grandfather has told her, have a mazal, a guardian angel, a celestial guide, who speaks up for them in heaven. Elvina feels she particularly needs a mazal because she is not an ordinary girl. She has been taught by her grandfather to read and write Hebrew, and trained by her mother in the use of medicinal plants. And she has a passion for writing. That, she feels, makes her really different.

Elvina is anxious and frightened. She dreams that she is Queen Esther. Maybe she will play a part in saving her people.

Miriam, Elvina's mother, and Precious, her grandmother, leave Troyes to care for her aunt, who is about to give birth in a small village. Elvina remains to keep house for her father, her grandfather, her brother, Yom Tov, and her cousin Samuel. When she has some free time, she attends the little boys' school because she likes to study, and because she likes the way the young and handsome master Obadiah explains the lessons, always quoting his own master, Elvina's beloved grandfather, Solomon ben Isaac.

One Sabbath afternoon, Elvina is at home with just one old servant. Three Crusaders push their way into the house. One of them, Gauthier, a boy barely older than Elvina, is wounded. Elvina has to think fast and conquer her terror. She expertly tends the boy's wound, as her mother has taught her, and while doing so, she listens to the men's conversation. To her horror, she realizes that they have taken Samuel and Yom Tov captive. She convinces the Crusaders to free them.

A few days later, she finds Gauthier hiding in a hole. He explains that he does not want to go on the Crusade and wishes instead to study in a monastery. He begs Elvina secretly to bring him food. In return, he promises to warn her if the Crusaders should decide to harm the Jews of Troyes. He will know because his brother visits him in his hiding place and keeps him informed. A friendship develops between Gauthier and Elvina.

Elvina has several friends, some who are Jewish (including the twins Naomi and Rachel, whom she secretly teaches to read) and some who are Christian (Marguerite and Jeanne, the daughters of a farmer). Relations with the Christian girls are sometimes difficult. "Why don't you just get baptized, then you would be like everybody else," they ask Elvina, much to her distress. Marguerite and Jeanne sometime accuse her of being a witch, all the while asking her for remedies.

Solomon ben Isaac plays an important part in Elvina's life. She turns to him whenever she is upset. But she doesn't tell anyone (except her mazal) that she is hiding a Crusader. This secret is a heavy burden and she feels increasingly guilty.

Purim arrives, and with Purim comes the full moon and a lunar eclipse. The eclipse is a bad omen for everybody but especially for the Jews, who could be accused of having caused "the moon's troubles." Elvina, in a paroxysm of guilt, imagines that she might be partly responsible for the eclipse and for whatever action the Crusaders might take against her people.

Obadiah has now heard that Elvina has been hiding a young Crusader. Outraged, he kicks her out of the school.

Elvina's father puts himself in danger in an attempt to protect the Jewish community by taking money to the Crusaders. Elvina is frantic with worry. When he returns, he tells how his life has been saved and his mission made possible by a young Crusader named Robert.

It soon becomes known that Robert has acted in gratitude for Elvina's kindness to his little brother, Gauthier. Thus Elvina has, indeed, saved her father's life and contributed to the safety of the Jews of Troyes.

The Crusaders leave Troyes without doing much harm.

Solomon ben Isaac personally takes Elvina back to the school, "recommends" her to Obadiah, and, though worried about his German brothers' fate at the hands of the Crusaders as they move east, expresses the hope that he will soon dance at his granddaughter's wedding . . .

Elvina's Mirror

Cast of Characters

Historical Characters

Elvina, Solomon ben Isaac's eldest granddaughter, left no writings but was well known for her wisdom and knowledge of Jewish Law and medical remedies. She is mentioned in a commentary of the Talmud.

Miriam, the eldest daughter of Solomon ben Isaac, was the wife of Judah ben Nathan and the mother of Elvina and Yom Tov.

Rachel, the youngest daughter of Solomon ben Isaac, was married and lived in Châlons.

Solomon ben Isaac was born in Troyes, France, in 1040. He studied for several years in the great Jewish academies of Mainz and Worms, in Germany. He then returned to Troyes, where he founded his own academy, or yeshivah, which became very famous. His precise and detailed commentaries of the Bible and the Talmud soon became so famous that Jews made copies of them to take wherever they traveled and settled. Today, both the Hebrew Bible and the Talmud are published with his commentaries printed in smaller characters below or alongside the text.

Solomon ben Isaac died in Troyes in 1105. He is known under the name of Rashi, which is the acronym of Rabbi Shlomo Yitzhaki, his Hebrew name.

Yochebed, the second daughter of Solomon ben Isaac, was the wife of Meir ben Samuel and the mother of Samuel and Isaac. (Some years later she gave birth to Jacob, the very famous Rabbenu Tam.) They lived in Ramerupt, a village not far from Troyes.

Fictional Characters

Columba, a young girl, is a refugee from Germany, where the Crusaders massacred many Jews the previous year.

Ephraim is Columba's cousin.

Fleurdelys and **Hannah** are the daughters of Yochebed.

Gauthier is a young Christian knight whom Elvina hid and helped the previous year, when he refused to become a Crusader.

Godolias is Columba's little brother.

Marguerite and **Jeanne**, Christian girls and friends of Elvina, are the daughters of **Master Hubert**, a rich farmer.

Muriel, a cousin of the twins Naomi and Rachel, is the daughter of **Flora**, who is Rosa's identical twin sister, and **Joseph ben Simon**.

Obadiah ben Moyses, Solomon ben Isaac's best student, is a schoolteacher.

Precious is the wife of Solomon ben Isaac.

Rachel and **Naomi**, the twins, are Elvina's best friends; they are the daughters of **Rosa** and **Jacob ben Reuben**.

Yakub ben Yussef and **Zakkariya**, his son, are Jewish merchants from Spain.

Zipporah is an old servant of the house of Solomon ben Isaac.

Chapter

1

It was late in the day when the heavy wagon rolled into the city of Troyes. It moved very slowly, pulled by a pair of oxen. A man and a boy, covered in cloaks and hoods, walked wearily alongside. They looked exhausted; their feet and legs, like those of the oxen, were caked in mud. The wagon hauled furniture, kitchen utensils, and other household goods piled haphazardly. Several muffled figures crouched on the wagon among bundles of clothes. The man urged on the oxen in a hoarse voice. The boy, his face hidden in his hood, kept silent.

In the streets around the synagogue the news spread from house to house, as people rushed to their doorsteps and windows to watch the strange, weary travelers pass by. Who were these travelers? They weren't traders for sure! Traders would be shouting out to announce their arrival. They would already be praising their wares from atop the wagon. But these travelers weren't saying anything at all. They didn't even greet the people they passed. Did they hope to go by unnoticed?

Two slim figures crossed Solomon ben Isaac's courtyard with light, quick steps. They ran, holding up the hems of their cloaks and skirts, not bothering to avoid the puddles left by the first downpour of spring. They hurried to the doorway on the left, which was wide open. Beside it, an old servant woman sat on a stool, poking at the fire under an iron tripod that held a huge steaming pot.

"Good afternoon, Zipporah. Your soup smells delicious! Where's Elvina?"

Zipporah looked at them with a sour expression. "Elvina is busy. She doesn't need two little scatterbrains coming to bother her."

"Naomi! Rachel!" A thirteen-year-old girl with dark brown braids appeared on the doorstep. She held a notebook made of several sheets of parchment sewn together, and she was blowing on one of the pages to dry the ink. The two "little scatterbrains" rushed up to her, grabbed her by the arms, and pulled her into the courtyard, dragging her into a circle dance.

Elvina laughed and pulled herself away from them. "Stop! You'll send my notebook flying into a puddle! Will you never be sensible? I can't believe you are eleven years old."

"What's this notebook? Show it to us!"

The twins pressed close to Elvina as she opened her notebook. "My grandfather, Solomon ben Isaac, gave me these sheets of parchment as a gift. They have some holes here and there but nothing too bad. I can easily write around them."

"Did you write all this?" asked Rachel.

"There are still some blank pages," Naomi remarked.

"Yes," answered Elvina. "I copy out the psalms I like best. That way I will have my own book of psalms. Little by little, I intend to build up my own personal library."

Together Rachel and Naomi asked, "Can we read from your notebook or is it too hard for us?"

"It's hard," Elvina answered, "but I'll read some verses with you. I'll translate them as I go along. Follow my finger: 'You wrap yourself as in a cloak. You unfold the heavens like a tapestry. Above the waters, you have raised the vaults of your sublime dwelling. The clouds serve you as a chariot. You ride on the wings of the wind.'"

The twins remained silent for a moment, then both exclaimed at the same time, "How beautiful!"

"This was the very first psalm I copied, because I like to look at the sky, as you know."

"How lucky you are. You can read it so easily."

This made Elvina laugh. "It isn't luck," she said. "I've been studying and working very hard, for years. But what are you two doing outside at this hour, anyway? You're not bringing bad news, I hope?"

The twins started speaking at the same time, as they always did.

"A strange group of people have just arrived in town, with their wagon."

"They're going through our neighborhood right now."

"Come and see for yourself!"

"If you don't, you'll be the only one!"

Elvina listened to them, then she asked, "How are this wagon and its passengers any concern of yours? It will soon be dark. Go home! Don't tell me you have nothing to do, with Passover only a week away."

The same look of disgust appeared on both plump-cheeked faces. "We've just spent the whole day washing, scrubbing, and sweeping up breadcrumbs to be ready for Pesach."

"Muriel has gone to visit our older sister Bella, who is going to have her baby very soon, you know, and . . ."

" . . . that makes more work for us."

Elvina interrupted them. "This strange group with the wagon, did you see them?"

"Not yet."

Naomi glanced over at Zipporah to make sure she couldn't hear, then said very softly, "Our aunt Flora saw them. She swears the wagon was led by ghosts."

Rachel whispered in the hollow of Elvina's ear, "She heard the man talk to the oxen. His voice wasn't human!"

Whispering into Elvina's other ear, Naomi explained, "He doesn't greet anyone, but he knows his way around perfectly. What else could he be but a . . ."

Elvina pushed both of them away and covered her ears with her hands. "Enough! I'm not listening to any more! My grandfather, Solomon ben Isaac, would be angry if he knew that I allowed you to repeat such nonsense."

Naomi, trying to look reasonable, said, "But if it happens to be a Jewish family coming to stay in our neighborhood, it would be a good deed to help them, wouldn't it?"

Rachel continued in the same reasonable tone, "Don't forget that we are your students. Well then, it seems to me we have a duty to help these people, *precisely* because night is coming on."

Elvina burst out laughing. "You don't know a thing about these travelers, not even if they plan to stop here, but now it's your duty to go help them. Why don't you just admit that you'll use any old excuse to go out? It's much more fun to go and meet some travelers than to help your mother and your aunt clean the house for Pesach!"

The twins laughed too, but then they stamped their feet impatiently. "We would already know who they are and where they are going if we hadn't been here forever, begging you to come with us! So, yes or no, are you coming?"

"You seem to forget that we began by reading some beautiful verses," Elvina reminded them. "But yes, I'm coming! Just let me put away my things and put on my cloak."

Rachel and Naomi threw their arms around Elvina's neck. They had grown nearly as tall as their friend.

Chapter

2

"Let's go down the alley. We'll catch up with them faster."

Arms entwined, the three girls started to walk along the alley leading to the school and the synagogue. The sky had cleared, and lovely pink clouds had formed, as often happened in the late afternoon.

Rachel sniffed the air. "Doesn't it smell wonderful? The blackthorns are in bloom. That should please you, Elvina."

Naomi added, nudging her friend, "You're very glad we came to look for you. Admit it!"

Elvina laughed and planted a kiss on Naomi's right cheek and on Rachel's left. "Yes, I'm very glad."

Along the way, doors were opening and women were coming out, hastily covering their heads and shoulders with their shawls—mistresses and servants, young and old, all bursting with curiosity. Together they reached the corner of the street where the synagogue stood. They began to hear the squeak of cart wheels and the sound of objects bouncing and knocking against each other.

"They've taken the road by the forge."

"Are they going to Dieulesault's house?"

They raised their skirts and ran. At the end of the street, as they were about to round the corner, they stopped cold. "There they are! In front of Jeremiah's house!"

The memory was still fresh of the winter night when Jeremiah the potter, driven to despair by the deaths of his wife and three children within a few days from the same fever, set fire to his own house. All of the women remembered the efforts of their husbands, fathers, and sons to put out the fire before it could spread to the other houses. At dawn, all that was left was a smoldering ruin. As for Jeremiah, he had disappeared without a trace.

One woman cried out, "Look! The man and the boy are carrying their things into the house."

Her neighbor added, "Moving into a house that is cursed. These people must be desperate."

"Aren't they afraid of the demons that haunt ruins?"

"That's right. There's She'iyyah, who takes the shape of an ox. My husband told me about him."

"Quiet! You're not supposed to say the names of demons!"

Rachel and Naomi huddled up against Elvina. Naomi whispered, "We told you they were no ordinary travelers."

Clinging to one another, the women stared at the oxen standing in front of what had once been Jeremiah's house—walls, some charred beams, a torn up roof.

A man's voice said, "You wouldn't catch me setting foot in that ruin."

The twins spun their heads around. "Uncle Joseph!" they cried.

Joseph ben Simon continued, "And I don't half like the looks of those animals. Stay close, girls. God forbid something bad should happen to you!"

Elvina wanted to point out that the oxen standing in front of poor Jeremiah's house seemed calm, tired out, and very ordinary; but out of respect for Joseph ben Simon, who was the father of her friend Muriel, she kept silent.

Several men and boys had come out of the synagogue. They saw the small crowd of curious people and joined them. Among them were Yom Tov, Elvina's younger brother, and Samuel ben Meir, their cousin. She tried to hide behind Joseph ben Simon, but the two boys had already spotted her.

"What are you doing here?" Yom Tov asked. "Do you want me to tell Father that you are hanging around in the street with a bunch of people who are conjuring up demons?"

Elvina had a strong urge to slap him. Instead, she said, "One would think the two of you came into the world for the sole purpose of spying on me. No one is conjuring anything. Go back to your studying and leave me alone."

Samuel shot back, "Grandfather would not be happy to find you here. You know perfectly well what he says: the less you speak of demons, the better off you are."

Elvina didn't answer. For once, her cousin was right. Samuel could feel her hesitating. He asked in a tone that was almost friendly, "Do you want us to walk you home?"

"No. I'll go back with our neighbors."

The two boys went on their way. A long evening of study lay ahead of them.

Elvina knew that it was her grandfather's custom to remain in the synagogue until the last of the men had finished reciting his prayers, so that no one would be left alone there at night. Would he come afterward, she wondered, to welcome these strange travelers?

In the dusk, she could still make out several muffled figures stirring about on the wagon. They must have been speaking among themselves, but she couldn't hear them. Why didn't they climb down? Ordinarily, the arrival of travelers was cause for celebration: people called out to each other, laughed, exchanged news . . .

The man and the boy went back and forth. They entered the ruin carrying bundles, or pieces of furniture, then came out, their heads bowed and hidden inside their hoods. They seemed not to notice the small crowd of men, women, and children watching their every move with a mixture of amazement and fear. Tongues were wagging.

"These people aren't poor. The poor do not own a big, four-wheeled wagon and a pair of oxen."

"When they passed in front of my place, I thought I saw some chests with shiny metal fittings. And trestles and planks and benches. And a cauldron that looked bigger than any we have here in Troyes."

"But if they are rich, why are they moving into that accursed house?"

To that question, no one had an answer. The sky had changed from pink to dark gray, and the sun had disappeared. All were silent now, keeping their distance. They gazed with horror at the ruin that seemed more sinister in the twilight, and at the wagon and oxen whose shapes became increasingly blurred. Suddenly Elvina cried, "There's my grandfather!"

A murmur ran through the group of men and women, who were riveted to their spot. "Solomon ben Isaac! At last!"

Elvina felt a surge of pride when she saw, once again, that the mere presence of Solomon ben Isaac was enough to reassure his people. She couldn't imagine what the world would be like without him. But as he approached at his usual steady, unhurried pace, Elvina's throat knotted up. He was no longer the grandfather of her early childhood, always going about with his head high, a mischievous or ironic smile on his lips. He now was a grandfather bowed down by worry and sorrow. His cloak looked too big on him. Walking beside him was Dieulesault, the blacksmith, who was as famous for his slowness in reciting his prayers as for his immense physical strength.

Elvina ran to meet Solomon. When he caught sight of her, he frowned. "What is my granddaughter doing here in the street, at this late hour, with this flock of idle folk? As far as I know, it isn't your habit to stand around staring at nothing."

"Isn't it the custom of our community to welcome travelers and offer help?" Elvina asked.

But Solomon ben Isaac did not answer her. He had already turned to address those who had formed a circle around them. "Are there no men here ready to help these people?"

Someone answered, "Master Solomon, it's not that we don't want to help. But you know what they say about ruins. Even our rabbis say so in the Talmud: if you go inside a ruin, you risk running into a demon."

Elvina, who could read every nuance of her grandfather's expression, saw that he was irritated, although he answered courteously, "This danger only applies to those who go in alone. That is not the case this evening. But night will soon fall. Dieulesault, have you done what I told you?"

The blacksmith nodded. "My brothers and I went in there yesterday. The beams are charred but solid. There is nothing to be afraid of."

"Good. Take two men with you. Unload the wagon as quickly as possible. Let these poor people and their animals have shelter for the night, at least. And now, let each of you go home."

Solomon ben Isaac had raised his voice enough to be heard by everyone. His tone did not allow for any further discussion. He took Elvina's hand. "Good night to all," he said.

Without letting go of her hand, he started off with long strides. Elvina had to hold up her skirt with the other hand in order to keep up. This was how he walked with her when she was little. Her grandfather's hand was firm and warm, but he was silent and seemed preoccupied.

Elvina was the one to speak. "Several of the travelers are women, I think. I could help them get settled, bring them supplies. They may not have any oil to light their lamps."

Without slowing down, Solomon answered, "Don't concern yourself about it."

Elvina kept quiet, but she was surprised and a little hurt. Ever since she was very small Solomon ben Isaac had always explained to her his decisions and orders. Finally she ventured to ask, "My grandfather doesn't consider me worthy to know more?"

Solomon shook his head. "Soon you will know everything. But for now, I'll say it again, do not concern yourself about that family."

When they reached the courtyard of their house, Elvina noticed that several stars had come out. A beautiful, clear, crescent moon was rising, brilliant in the silvery sky. An owl hooted. The first watch of the night was about to begin. One more week and the moon would be full. One more week and it would be Pesach.

Chapter

3

*T*o my dear, sweet aunt Rachel,

   May the Holy One bless you and protect you and grant that we see you again soon. My grandfather has asked me to write to you that we are all in good health, thank God, and that we love you. We miss you terribly, I especially, your poor gazelle who now sleeps alone and no longer has her confidant to comfort her and reassure her at night when she is sad or worried. At least, this past winter, I was not expected to hatch eggs in my apron. My father has resigned himself to the fact that he has a daughter who is not like other girls.

   A year ago, we were preparing for Pesach with joy and relief, as Peter the Hermit's troops had left our region without harming us. This year, in spite of our efforts to be joyful, it is with sadness that we are getting ready to celebrate Pesach because we know that our Jewish brothers and sisters in Germany have met with a terrible fate at the hands of the Crusaders. I saw the tears streaming down my grandfather's cheeks each time he received news from Mainz or Worms.

   Tomorrow morning, a messenger is leaving for Châlons. He will be carrying several responsa from my grandfather to the leaders of your community, this letter for you, and . . . guess what? A few "responsa" from your gazelle. My grandfather has kept his promise to give me every possible opportunity to satisfy what he calls my fondness for writing. As he is too busy to answer all of the letters he receives at this time of year, inquiring about preparations for Passover, he has asked me—yes, me!—to reply to some of the letters written to him by ladies from distant Jewish communities. Your gazelle now carries on an official correspondence!

   Dear, sweet aunt Rachel, when will I see you again? This messenger is so lucky. How I would love to jump on a horse and bring you my letter!

*T*o the very honorable lady Judith,

    I am answering on behalf of our master Solomon ben Isaac, who is my grandfather. You had your scribe write that in your village all of the Jewish families share one oven, and that the women argue and even get into fights when comes the time to cook the Pesach matzot, *so that the* matzot *either burn or aren't cooked enough. Our master Solomon ben Isaac has instructed me to pass on to you the solution given by our sages. Three women can work by the oven at the same time as long as they don't begin at the same moment. While one is putting her* matzot *in the oven, the second one is shaping hers, and the third one is kneading her dough. This way the dough does not sit too long, there is no risk of it fermenting, and everything will go well, without any arguing. What will your Christian neighbors think if they see the pious daughters of Israel pulling each other's hair out and scratching each other's faces while preparing for the most beautiful holiday of the whole year? Just think! How shameful!*

---

*T*o the very honorable Lady Prisca,

    A young and unimportant member of Solomon ben Isaac's household has the honor of answering, following his instructions, the letter written him by Eliezer, your children's teacher. Eliezer ben Simon will read you this response. You wish to give your children something to eat during the afternoon before the seder because your motherly heart can't stand listening to the children crying and complaining that they are hungry. Eliezer ben Simon, who is young and anxious to do the right thing, thinks it is his duty to prevent you from feeding the children. True, you should be hungry for the Pesach meal. However, Solomon ben Isaac, my grandfather, allows his students and his family to eat fruit and vegetables and even a little meat, which give you an appetite. But no oatmeal or bread. They would fill the stomach. The children need to be happy and wide awake without being drowsy from too much food. When they come to the table, they must want to ask questions and to learn why, on that night, everything is different. You can also give them a light snack of walnuts and apples.

    In our family, we have a tradition of eating a little leek and turnip soup, and, for dessert, walnuts fried in honey, which my grandfather particularly enjoys. This way, everyone feels well, the children do not have stomach-aches, and our appetites are sharpened. We must be hungry when we eat the bread of affliction, which reminds us that we were slaves in Egypt.

Chapter

4

A bit of light filtered through the green cloth hanging over the window. It was cold in the room, but it was no longer the dark and gloomy cold of winter. It was a sharp, bright cold, promising a beautiful, clear day. A rooster crowed. Elvina stretched and rolled over. In a little while, she thought, we shall praise the Lord for having made the rooster smart enough to tell day from night, but our rooster is much too smart; he puts his pride in beating Simha the *shammash* to it, and Simha puts his pride in beating the rooster to it. Today the smart rooster won. Elvina laughed to herself and swung her legs up in the air. "The legs of a gazelle," Aunt Rachel used to say. Rachel, Rachel, sweet little aunt Rachel, where are you? Why aren't you here laughing with me?

The smell of fire and boiling oatmeal reached Elvina's nostrils. She wondered if she would get up right away, or wait until Simha came pounding on the window shutters, despicable Simha whose name means joy, the joy of waking up people who would rather sleep.

"Elvina! Get up! I need you to run to the apothecary's. Hurry! I want leeches to put on your father."

As soon as she heard her mother's voice, Elvina hastily thanked the Almighty for restoring her soul and jumped from the bed.

"What's wrong with him?"

Miriam handed Elvina a pitcher of water and a small basin. While Elvina quickly washed her hands, her mother stated in a very loud voice, to ward off the evil spirits, "Judah ben Nathan is perfectly healthy."

But then she whispered, "He has a little fever. Get washed, get dressed, and eat some oatmeal before you go out. I don't want you to catch cold, too. These first days of spring are treacherous."

She watched Elvina getting dressed. Her eye was critical. "Won't you ever get rid of this fur vest? It's much too small for you. You could give it to your cousin Fleurdelys. Take my cloak if you are cold."

13

Elvina didn't answer. She buried her nose in the long rabbit hair, which still kept a little of her aunt Rachel's familiar smell. A year had passed since that day when Rachel, just before leaving for Châlons, had given her the vest to wear under her dress on very cold days. Now the vest was too tight and crushed her chest. But so what? Every time she put it on she felt wrapped in the warmth and tenderness that her beloved aunt had lavished on her.

Miriam smoothed Elvina's hair and braided it, one braid on each side. Elvina closed her eyes, enjoying the gentleness of her mother's hands. This was a rare pleasure, now, having her mother braid her hair. It suddenly seemed to Elvina that she was a very small girl again. She allowed herself to go a little limp.

"Do you remember," she asked, "when I was small, how I used to love looking at myself in your eyes? I would see a tiny Elvina with dark braids and a rather long face, and it made me laugh. And you always told me that there is no better mirror for a girl than her mother's eyes."

She opened her eyes: Miriam's eyes were filled with tears. "What is it? Did I say something that made you sad?"

"No. But I miss Rachel just as much as you do. And I'm doubly sad because I know my little sister is unhappy."

"Then why, why doesn't she come back? Is a woman obliged to stay with a mean husband?"

Miriam put her fingers on Elvina's lips and kissed her. "Hush. Go, now."

Elvina ran downstairs. No one was there. On the table, the big bowl in which Zipporah had served oatmeal to the boys was empty. Next to the bowl stood a jug full of water.

"Zipporah, was this water drawn from the well this morning?" Elvina asked.

Zipporah appeared, her head wrapped up in a dark scarf. Except for her long skinny nose, not much of her face could be seen. She slammed down a full bowl in front of Elvina. "Do you think I don't know evil spirits are attracted to water that has been left standing all night, and that they swim on it like ducks on a pond? A thirteen-year-old girl has something to teach me? The water has just been drawn, while you were lolling about in your bed."

The market was hopping when Elvina reached the street where the Jewish merchants had their shops. Only five days were left before Pesach! And the Sabbath was tomorrow night! If she hadn't been so worried about her father, Elvina would have been thrilled to go into the apothecary's cramped little shop, where a strange bitter smell grabbed her and tickled her throat, and then became rather pleasant after she got used to it.

The apothecary was a fat man whose face disappeared behind a thick red beard. He was squatting on a low stool, busily weighing grasshopper eggs on a tiny scale. His fingers were thick, but his gestures were precise and delicate. As soon as he saw Elvina, he let go of his scale, first making sure it was perfectly balanced and nothing would fall off it.

"These grasshopper eggs are the best remedy for earaches," he said, "but they cost me an arm and a leg. The Spanish merchant who brings them to me only comes twice a year. These are the eggs of large desert grasshoppers, mind you, not your common little green grasshopper that we have in our fields. The same Spaniard sold me several bunches of madder plants. You tie one of these bunches to the neck of a person who has sunk into melancholy and the next thing you know, the sadness has gone away. But Elvina, it's not often that you honor me with a visit! Did your mother send you, so early in the morning? Usually she only uses the plants and herbs she herself picks. Tell me, what does she need today?"

"Leeches."

"Leeches? For whom does she need them?"

"For my father."

"For Judah ben Nathan? Is he . . . ?"

Elvina looked him straight in the eye. "My father is perfectly healthy," she said in a loud voice. "But we need leeches."

The apothecary bowed politely. "I understand. I don't have any here, but the pond where I get them is close by, and I'll send my son over there right now. By the time you finish the rest of your shopping, I should have at least half a dozen of them for you. And while you're here, if Judah ben Nathan has a headache, it so happens that just this morning I boiled a pigeon in vinegar. Then I mixed the vinegar with rose oil. There is nothing like it to cure headaches . . ."

Elvina shook her head. "My mother only wants leeches."

She went back out into the street. It was bustling with people, but the crowds of housewives were less noisy, less cheerful than in previous years.

"Elvina!"

Two identical women walked up to her. Their big smiles revealed their gums. They were so identical that they were actually missing the same teeth. Flora was Muriel's mother. Rosa, her twin sister, was the mother of Bella and the twins, Naomi and Rachel. Flora and Rosa were almost always seen together ever since Rosa, Jacob ben Reuben, and their children had come to live in town. Before that they had lived on their farm. But last year, after the Crusaders beat Jacob ben Reuben and stole all his sheep, they were too scared to remain on the farm. Jacob sold it to Christians who had been wanting it for a long time. Now he worked with his cousin, Nathan ben Simon, the tanner.

Rosa and Flora kissed Elvina. "We are getting ready for Pesach," Rosa said. "But our hearts aren't in it. Nothing is the way it used to be. We actually have to buy meat for our own lamb stew. To think we used to provide it for others, and the best quality, too!" She was close to tears. "This would be lambing season," she sniffled. "I think about it all the time. All the little lambs."

She wiped her nose with her sleeve and managed a smile. "Come on over to our house, Elvina, you know the girls love you like a sister. And also . . ." She leaned toward Elvina and whispered, "you teach them so many things. They show me their wax tablets, sometimes, when their father is not around, and I too am learning to read. I can recognize several characters!"

But Elvina was thinking about her father. "I have to run home as soon as I get my leeches. My mother is waiting for me."

The biggest crowd was in front of the spice merchant's shop. But this year, he was not crying out about the quality of his spices, saying that they came straight from the Holy Land. This would have reminded everyone of the passage of the Crusaders, on their way to the Holy Land, exactly a year before. Anyway, there was no need to brag about his merchandise or call out to the housewives. He was the only one selling the products needed to make the *haroset*: figs, dates, nuts, and spices. No good Jewish housewife could avoid him.

As always, his donkey was tied in front of the shop. The women jostled him and bumped into him as they tried to get closer to the stall. He fought back by pushing them a little with his head. Elvina stroked his long ears. "Poor little donkey," she whispered into one of them. "Be patient! This won't last!"

The smell of cinnamon, honey, and almond oil filled the air in front of the shop. Elvina remembered she needed ginger for her *haroset*. She pushed her way into the shop, up to the table where sacks full of spices were neatly lined up.

All of a sudden, right next to Elvina's shoulder, a small, clear, flutelike voice spoke out a little hesitantly. "I would like two pieces of cinnamon bark, and also a ginger root, not too big. And some figs and dates."

The words were pronounced correctly in good French, but slowly, in a way that reminded Elvina of some of her grandfather's visitors from distant lands. A little girl, about ten years old, was handing the merchant two leather pouches for him to put the figs and the dates in. The face of the girl was delicate, her eyes very black, and her hair almost blond. Elvina had never seen her before.

To Elvina's great surprise, the merchant looked coldly at his young customer. "I can pay," the girl added, speaking fast, in a kind of whisper.

The merchant grabbed the two pouches and, instead of his usual "Ginger for this lovely girlie. Coming right up, sweetheart, and while you wait, won't you taste one of my dates, go ahead, my pleasure . . . ," he snapped at the girl, "So, you folks are getting ready for Pesach? Who would have thought?" His tone was mean and sarcastic. Elvina had never heard him speak that way.

The little girl turned very pale and did not respond. Several women burst out laughing. One of them nudged Elvina and said out loud, "She's the daughter of those people who have moved into Jeremiah's house, or what's left of it."

Another woman spoke up. "Everybody knows now why they came to Troyes. Hiding their shame, that's what. They're Jews who allowed themselves to be baptized."

The girl stuffed her purchases into her sleeve, spun around, and ran out without looking at anyone. The women moved away from her.

Only once in her life had Elvina seen a crowd moving back in this way from a fellow creature. Then, the person in question was a leper whose eyes were as red as embers and whose nose had been eaten away by the disease. Today, women Elvina had known her entire life, women who had always smiled at her, hugged her, and said nice things to her, were stepping away from a pretty little girl, deathly pale and on the verge of tears, just as they would have done if she had been a leper.

M y dear Mazal, my guardian angel, are you getting tired of speaking up for me?

Today I'm afraid I gave in to my regrettable habit of not minding my own business. When I finally came out again from the apothecary's shop, with four disgusting fat leeches squirming in their jar, I heard the fruit seller yelling, "Take your two apples and get out of here! And I don't want your money!"

Just as they had done in the spice merchant's shop, the women stepped away from the little stranger and stared at her, revulsion on their faces. At first she walked bravely down the street, holding her head high, looking straight ahead of her. I really admired her courage. But as soon as she thought no one was looking at her any more, her courage abandoned her. She buried her face in her hands and started sobbing, right there, at the corner of Market Street and Forge Street. Her shoulders were shaking.

Mazal, my Mazal, you know me. I didn't stop to think. I rushed up to her, I told her not to cry, that surely things would come out all right. I put down my leeches and ginger and picked up her two apples, which had rolled on the ground. I couldn't pull her hands away from her face, so I hugged her. She barely comes up to my chin. Her hair was clean but smelled of smoke from the charred beams of poor Jeremiah's house. While I waited for her to calm down, I thought that I had never had to endure what she was enduring this morning. I have always lived in Troyes, which is my birthplace, even if it is the land of our exile. I have always been surrounded by kind, familiar faces. Wherever I go, everyone smiles at me, everyone greets me with respect and love as "the granddaughter of our master Solomon ben Isaac."

Finally she stopped crying. I patted her cheeks dry with my sleeve, and I asked her what her name was.

"Columba."

"What a pretty name. I'm Elvina. Where are you from?" I asked.

She hesitated for a moment. She looked all around us to make sure nobody was listening. There was no one. "From Mainz," she hiccupped.

I thought of the man and boy I had seen guiding the wagon. "You came with your father and your brother?"

"Yes. And also my mother, my little brother, and our servant."

"How come you're the one doing the shopping?" I asked.

"My mother is too busy. She is helping my father and my brother fix up the house."

She seemed worried all of a sudden, as if she was afraid she had revealed too much. "I have to go home," she said. "They are waiting for me."

I told her I also had to go home and that we would meet again. I had not noticed the old beggar: he had crawled right up to the street corner and had grabbed my jar. He was admiring my leeches, sticking out his tongue at them, and drooling, as he always does when he is not talking. When I tried to take my jar back, he held it tight, and laughed his stupid laugh. "What will you give me in return, missy?"

"What do you want? Hurry! I don't have all day."

"That's what you say. But if you have time for the pretty little stranger, you have time for me!"

"Tell me what you want. Quick! Where does it hurt, today?"

"My stomach. I've eaten too much. The housewives are giving me all the bread and cakes they have to get rid of before Pesach, you see . . ."

"Come by our house. I'll make you some herb tea. But give me back my leeches."

He grinned and pointed his finger at poor Columba, who was staring at him in horror.

"This little girl is proud," he said. "She's not telling you everything. She's not telling you that yesterday the women chased away her mother when she tried to cook her *matzot* in the communal oven. Nobody sees the old drooling idiot of a beggar, but he sees and hears many things."

I turned toward Columba. She had flushed to the roots of her hair. The look on her face was no longer one of horror but one of hate as she stared at the old beggar, who was drooling and rolling his eyeballs again.

"Is this true?" I asked her.

"Yes."

Then she ran away.

And then, Mazal, what did I do? I went home and gave the leeches to my mother, who ran back upstairs to my father's bedside. I took a large handful of flour from the hutch, packed it up in a piece of sackcloth, and ran to fetch Naomi and Rachel. I wanted them to come with me to the communal oven. I could not use my family's oven, and I had to work very fast, so I needed their help.

The twins invited me into their house. They had mysterious looks on their faces. "How lucky that you came over. We have something to show you."

"Couldn't you bring it to my house?" I asked.

"No. We were afraid of carrying it on our persons. You'll see why."

Naomi disappeared for a moment, then she returned and handed me a very thin strip of parchment. On each side there was an inscription written in the sacred language.

"We can understand one of the sides perfectly. It says, 'The sun shall be dark when it rises and the moon shall not cause its light to shine.' But on the other side, the only word we recognize is the word 'houses.'"

They were observing my face to see how I would react. "Well? You're our teacher. Can you tell us what it means?"

"It means something like: 'Beasts shall lie down there, and the houses shall be filled with owls.' These are verses from the prophet Isaiah. I heard them being read at the synagogue. Where did you find this parchment?"

"It was stuck in the post of our door."

"We couldn't wait to show it to you, but we didn't want to carry it with us."

"It wasn't rolled up like an amulet, and these verses don't look like they would protect a person. Actually, they look like they might even bring us bad luck."

As usual, the twins spoke at the same time. I told them they had done the right thing and I took the parchment. Then I asked them to come with me to the communal oven. All I said to them was that we would be doing a good deed. Rosa and Flora, the identical mothers, were too busy to notice the girls leaving the house. The communal kitchen is right near the synagogue and the school, but luckily no one in either place saw us.

There was a crowd in the communal kitchen, and it was stifling hot. Three of the women were covered with flour. The first was kneading the dough, the second was shaping the *matzot*, and the third was watching over the baking. Other women were waiting, sitting on a bench, chatting away. Their faces were gleaming with sweat. As soon as they saw me, they started nudging each other and winking at me.

"Elvina. What a lovely surprise. Why are you here?"

"I want to bake a few *matzot* for an old woman who is sick. Our own oven has not been lit up yet," I lied.

They all burst out laughing. "Poor old woman! Poor little sick old woman!"

Simonet's wife was there. She looks like a ferret, and even has the high-pitched voice of a ferret. "You will be disappointed, Elvina," she screeched, "you got here too late!"

"Too late for what?" I had no idea what she was talking about.

The little black ferret eyes were shining and her snout was wiggling, yes, I'm sure her nose was wiggling, as she replied, "We don't know any sick old woman. But we do know a handsome young school teacher who is most brave and learned, and who just left us to return to his classroom. Your grandfather sent him here to make sure everything was being done correctly. You just missed him. What a pity."

They continued laughing and joking, but those who were waiting for the oven let us take their turn. Simonet's wife kept repeating in that screechy voice of hers, "What the granddaughter of our master Solomon ben Isaac does is well done."

It took us very little time to bake three smallish *matzot*, which is as many as you can bake at once in the communal oven.

I sent Naomi and Rachel home, instructing them not to mention the parchment to a soul. And not to speak of houses filled with owls. I told them I would keep the parchment and later, after Pesach, we would decide what needed to be done. As I slipped the three *matzot* into one of my sleeves, I remembered what Gauthier used to say: "Women are always hiding things in their sleeves—that's what those wide sleeves are for."

I knew the ferret and her gossipy crowd would be spying on me. If they saw me walk to the school, they would never suspect what my real plan was.

Chapter

6

The school door creaked, as always, and Elvina thought Obadiah would do well to oil its old rusty hinges. The thought made her want to laugh. "Am I the mistress of the house, to be worrying about this old worm-eaten door?" She entered into the narrow hallway. A low stool was waiting for her. The stool was convenient for writing, much better than the pile of straw that used to be there. The stool seemed to be answering Elvina's question: "Yes, you have your place here, yes, you are the mistress of this house. No other girl or woman ever sets foot in the school."

That was certainly true, thought Elvina. She no longer had to slip in like a frightened mouse, hiding under her hood, and trying to make herself invisible. She had her place here. But she had come to listen to the lessons, not to worry about the squeaky hinges or the resin torches that smoked and stank.

Elvina sat down, reached into her sleeve, and took out her wax tablet and her ivory stylus, which she always carried with her. Actually, she hardly took any notes any more because Obadiah's explanations were familiar to her.

One of the boys had turned around. With his shoulder he pushed his neighbor, who also turned around. Elvina nodded and smiled pleasantly. There was nothing for the boys to do but bend their heads again over their parchments and their tablets. Last year, each boy wanted to be the first to spot the presence of "the girl" and point her out to the others, for the fun of watching Yom Tov and Samuel turn green with rage. But now that Samuel and Yom Tov were in the big school, there was no fun in it anymore.

All Elvina could see of Obadiah ben Moyses, the young schoolmaster, who was one of Solomon ben Isaac's best students, was his mane of black hair, black as a crow's wing. He was squatting in front of the boys, as always, because he liked to be at the same level as his students, who all sat on the floor. Now and then, he raised his stick and twirled it in the air, above the boys' heads. Surely he did that just to liven things up; Elvina had never seen him hit a student.

Obadiah pretended he hadn't noticed Elvina coming in. It was his habit, and it was as it should be.

The schoolroom was buzzing. It was as if all of the boys were stimulated by the brisk puffs of air coming into the room through the two windows, a cool spring air filled with the fragrance of the blooming blackthorn trees, reminding everyone that Passover was not far off.

The boys were reading and translating the passages of the Torah that tell of how the Almighty took the Jews out of Egypt where they were slaves. Obadiah had copied the passages on pieces of parchment so that the boys could learn them by heart. "Tomorrow evening, the last Sabbath before Pesach begins, and the day after tomorrow, during the morning service, our master Solomon ben Isaac will explain those passages. If you work hard today, you will be able to follow and understand his explanations," he told them.

The older boys sang the passages of the sacred text. The melody helped them memorize the verses. The younger boys read the passages word by word with the help of their teacher. When they seemed tired, he encouraged them. "Read slowly. Pronounce each syllable correctly. When we read the Torah, we must not stutter or stumble. Do you know what our sages say? They say that the words of the Torah are cups made of pure gold. They are very beautiful and precious and hard to come by, but they are also—and that is what makes it a miracle—fragile cups of glass, which break very easily."

The children sat absolutely still. Elvina could imagine the little ones gazing at Obadiah, their eyes wide open with wonder. One of them repeated, "Gold cups?"

"Yes. You are in the process of acquiring beautiful gold cups. But be careful! Those cups break just like glass cups! Come! Follow with your finger and show me the word you are reading. Then we will translate. Then you will learn to sing the verses, like the older boys are doing. And you will never forget them!"

Several shrill voices slowly made out the Hebrew words and Obadiah translated, "Seven days you shall eat unleavened bread; on the very first day you shall remove leaven from your houses."

"Do you understand?" Obadiah asked.

His question was met with a dismayed silence. Several boys were scratching themselves. Some discreetly pulled down their hoods, hoping to become invisible. Obadiah repeated his question. "Does everyone understand what we have just been reading?"

A very small voice murmured, "No."

"Say that again, louder! You don't understand?"

The small voice repeated, "I don't understand."

"Stand up!"

The boy got up, shaking and flushed. He was about seven years old. Obadiah went to him and, placing his hand on his head, said, "You don't understand. Good! Very good!"

Elvina smiled. How many times had she heard her grandfather speak in this very same way to his older students, some of whom were themselves teachers like Obadiah.

Obadiah smiled, too. It seemed to Elvina that he had glanced at her, but she wasn't sure. She already knew what he would say next.

"Why am I congratulating our friend Jacob? Because the student who reads without understanding is not a good student. Jacob has shown himself to be the best student among you because he alone was brave enough to admit he didn't understand. Now, let's see. What holiday are we reading about?"

Six high-pitched voices yelled, "Pesach!"

"Excellent. What is leaven?"

"It's what makes the dough rise when my mother is baking bread."

"Very good. And how do we make it disappear from our houses?"

"We hunt for all the crumbs, we sweep every corner of the house with feathers."

"Now, who can explain the word *matzot*?"

"I can!" claimed a chubby boy who belonged to the intermediate group. He sat cross-legged on a beautiful thick piece of blanket, which the other boys envied him.

His neighbors whispered loud enough for the whole class to hear, "If you can eat it, count on Jacquet to know what it is!"

"Silence!" Obadiah ordered. "Jacquet, tell us what it means."

"The *matzot* are pancakes made without leaven. You have to knead the dough very fast, make it into round flat shapes very fast, and bake them very fast."

All the boys burst out laughing. "And eat them very fast, because they taste awful!"

Obadiah stretched out his hands and the class became quiet again. "You have to make them so fast that the dough doesn't rise. Why?"

"Because the Jews had to leave Egypt very quickly," said one boy.

"The children of Israel had to take away their dough wrapped up in their cloaks," ventured another one.

"Right," approved Obadiah. "So now, Jacquet, can you recite the passage for us?"

Jacquet wriggled a bit, scratched his head, and mumbled, "I forget."

His neighbors hit him on the head. "Jacquet has eaten bread that was nibbled by the mice!"

"Or maybe by the cat!"

"Jacquet will eat anything. Every morning he rushes to eat any old bread that has been sitting around, even if the mice have nibbled at it. And bread nibbled by mice makes you forget everything."

All the boys laughed. Elvina, too, laughed in her sleeve. Even Obadiah was struggling hard not to burst out laughing, and he almost— but only almost—managed to sound very strict as he said, "Enough! Who wants to recite?"

"I do, master."

A big boy named Bonfils stood up and chanted in the sacred language, "And they baked unleavened cakes of the dough that they had taken out of Egypt, for it was not leavened, since they had been driven out of Egypt and could not delay."

The little boys were open-mouthed with admiration. Bonfils's chanting had been flawless. He had neither stuttered nor stumbled.

Obadiah smiled. "Very good. The day after tomorrow, in the synagogue, our master Solomon ben Isaac will explain that the children of Israel did not say to themselves: 'How can we go forth into the desert without provisions? What shall we eat?' They had faith in the Almighty and they left without provisions."

The youngest boy of the class, Toby ben Nathan, who had been attending school for only two weeks and was just beginning to read, asked, "Why is Bonfils swaying when he chants?"

Obadiah smiled again. "That's a very interesting question! Bonfils, can you answer?"

"We sway to remind ourselves that the children of Israel, who were about to receive the Law at the foot of Mount Sinai, trembled when they saw the smoke coming from the mountain."

Elvina put her tablet back into her sleeve. Today's lesson was one any girl who had to prepare for Pesach knew by heart! Hidden in her other sleeve, the three *matzot* now felt heavy, as she remembered Solomon ben Isaac's words, "Do not concern yourself about that family!"

Chapter 7

*T*he very respectable Lady Fleurette has asked her son to write us to inquire about the preparation of pots and pans and other utensils for Passover. A very young and humble member of Solomon ben Isaac's family has the
honor of replying on his behalf, as he is very busy. The messenger will soon be
on his way; his horse is already standing in our courtyard. He has letters to
carry to several villages before the beginning of the Sabbath.

All metal objects, dishes, pots, knives, goblets, and also wooden dishes
must be plunged into boiling water. In our family, this happens two days before
Pesach, and we make it a real party for the women and girls of our neighborhood. We (by now you have guessed that your correspondent belongs to the
female sex) set an enormous cauldron in the middle of our courtyard, which is
the biggest courtyard in the neighborhood, and we fill it with water. My mother
feeds a huge fire under the cauldron and makes sure the water never stops boiling. We plunge our plates, pots, knives, ladles, and goblets into the cauldron.
Then we chase the men and boys out of the courtyard and we use the water to
wash our clothes, our wimples, our scarves, and also our hair. We want to be
beautiful and clean for the holiday! We rinse each other using big ladles. Of
course we do this around noon, when the sun is hot, even if there is a little cool
spring wind blowing. While our hair dries, we eat cakes and drink a pitcher of
wine. If we are cold, we sing and dance. It is one more way for us, daughters of
Israel, to celebrate our coming out of Egypt where we were slaves.

Chapter

8

Simha the *shammash* didn't see anything when he came to knock on the shutters, but he was not carrying his torch, since it was the Sabbath. Zipporah, who usually went out to draw water from the well the moment the skies began to grow pale, didn't see anything, because she didn't draw water on the Sabbath. Judah ben Nathan, who had already gone off to the synagogue, didn't see anything, but then he never did see anything, everybody knew that.

A little later, Elvina went out to enjoy the peace of this morning of rest, to watch the sky become pink, and to breathe in the spring air. Whatever the season, she always loved the silence of the Sabbath morning in the Jewish neighborhood. Kitchen utensils weren't being dashed against one another, merchants weren't yelling at their horses or their donkeys to make them move faster, the blacksmiths weren't hammering in the forge. No one was poking at a fire, or throwing out pails of evil-smelling water into the street.

The hens were clucking peacefully. A ewe was bleating and her lamb answered her with his own tiny bleating, which sounded just like the cry of a newborn baby. And birds, birds were everywhere! Chirping and warbling and inviting Elvina to something vague but happy and beautiful.

The light was no longer the light of winter. The coolness of the morning stung Elvina's cheeks and hands, but it was not the kind of freezing cold that made her want to run back into the house and warm up by the stove. Quite the opposite.

Her grandparents' window was open. A smell of spicy meat stew floated to Elvina's nostrils. No woman in the neighborhood could compete with the Sabbath stew prepared by her grandmother, Precious. Not even her daughters! Elvina smiled to herself. Her grandfather was probably reading before setting off for the synagogue. He read for pleasure, from his beautiful book of midrashim, the rabbinic legends he loved so much.

If she were still a little girl, Elvina would run and snuggle against him to marvel once more at the book with its elegant script, a rare Spanish cursive script, then, together, they would read a legend. Perhaps the one about the marriage of King Solomon's daughter with a young man hidden in an ox carcass brought to her by a vulture.

Elvina wondered. Had she become someone else? A new Elvina who preferred to stay alone this morning, alone in the courtyard, offering up her cheeks to the crisp morning air, which made her skin feel tingly and alive, after the endless winter months during which she forgot she even had a skin?

Elvina shook her hair, which she had not braided. She stretched out her arms and wiggled her fingers. She twirled around a little. Today is the Sabbath, she thought. I am grown up now. I shouldn't be dancing! But she felt free and happy and full of life, in her new dress of a deep blue color. She was wearing it without a belt. She thought, "I will not wear my cloak to go to the synagogue. The weather is too beautiful, my cloak is too heavy and I want to feel light on my feet!"

Suddenly she saw the cat. He was lying full length on the ground, his legs stretched out in front of him, up against the wall of the chicken coop, almost out on the street. She called out to him, "Well, Cat, sleeping in, this morning? Aren't you going to come and rub yourself against my legs? You've eaten so many mice you can't move any more?"

She crossed the courtyard, bent down, and screamed. The cat's throat had been slit. The head was almost severed from the body, the neck was one huge open wound, and flies were buzzing around it, the first of the season. The ground was dark and wet, soaked in blood. Elvina screamed again, then she ran toward the door, which had already opened, and Solomon was running out toward his granddaughter.

Chapter

9

azal, dear Mazal, I owe you many thanks. I'm sure you inspired me to go out first thing in the morning so I would find the cat and my grandfather would have time to put it in a bag and carry it—although it was the Sabbath—into his house before anyone else could see it. Yes, Solomon ben Isaac violated the Sabbath! There had to be a very serious reason, and I had guessed it even before he explained it to me. It was most important to prevent the non-Jews from discovering the cat because they might have accused us Jews of sorcery. What kind of sorcery, I have no idea, but I could see that it worried my grandfather. By acting fast to avoid any possibility of such an accusation we may have saved lives! We know what happened last year to our brothers and sisters of the German communities. This evening, as soon as the Sabbath was over, Dieulesault came and took away the bag containing the cat. He will bury it during the night in a corner of his forge. It was also most important to avoid a panic among the Jews. A cat practically decapitated in the courtyard of a Jewish family on the Sabbath. What does it mean? Is it a threat? Who would want to threaten us?

Mazal, Mazal, I can see that once again my grandfather is sad and preoccupied, and so is my father. My grandmother cries and wrings her hands. She is fully expecting our Christian neighbors to come and burn our houses. My father has instructed me to keep absolutely quiet about the dead cat. I can't mention it to anyone. So, as I try to fall asleep, I'm talking to you, my dear Mazal.

Tomorrow, my uncle Meir, my aunt Yochebed, and their children are arriving. May the Almighty grant them a safe trip. I can already hear Zipporah, who is always on the alert, calling out, "Here they come! Here is our mistress Yochebed and here is our master Meir ben Samuel! And here are the dear children!"

We will all run out to help them climb down from my uncle's magnificent new wagon, which we have not yet seen, but I've heard he is very proud of it. My aunt Yochebed will hand over little Hannah to my mother, who will smother her with kisses. "What an ugly child!" she will exclaim, to ward off the evil eye. "She hasn't grown at all since the last time I saw her." To which my aunt will reply, of course, "She gives me nothing but trouble." Samuel and Yom Tov will feed sweets to the horses, good old horses that are part of the family. Then my father, who has completely recovered from his fever and doesn't cough anymore, thank God, will take the horses to Simonet's stable, since we have neither horses nor a stable.

Then my grandfather will arrive, rushing home from the synagogue. He will bless his daughter, his son-in-law, and each child in turn, taking their heads between his two hands. He will kiss my aunt Yochebed and pinch the cheeks of my cousins, Fleurdelys, who is seven, and Isaac, who is four. He will lift up Hannah in his arms and spin her in the air as he does with all of his grandchildren as long as they are light enough for him to do it, and Hannah will pull his beard. My mother and my aunt Yochebed, who haven't seen each other for months and months, will kiss and hug at least a thousand times. My mother will help her sister unravel her headscarf. They will stare at each other to see if they have changed. They'll touch each other's faces with their fingers and cry a little, and speak very fast in a language of their own, as if they were little girls again. And I will wish I had a sister. So I will take Fleurdelys into my arms and help her wash her face because she will certainly be covered with dust after the long trip. And while I help Fleurdelys, my aunt Yochebed will run all over the courtyard, sit on the bench, get up again, exclaim that everything is different, no, everything is the same, and again she and my mother will laugh and cry and kiss, and each one will admire the other's dress, even if their dresses are exactly alike, made of dark gray wool.

My grandmother will sob, as she never fails to do on great occasions. To comfort her, my uncle Meir will tell her that just before starting on the trip he dreamed of a galloping white horse, and that it is a good omen.

How I wish they were already here! I want to see Uncle Meir's new wagon pulling into our courtyard at this very moment and hear Zipporah's joyful cry. I want to hear Uncle Meir telling us about his dream as he gets off his horse.

If only there had not been the slaughtered cat this morning!

And, tomorrow morning, before they arrive, I must find a way of getting the *matzot* to Columba's family without anybody noticing. Dear Mazal, do you think maybe you could help me?

Chapter

10

Sunday morning. Passover would begin tomorrow evening and there was still so much to do. After the morning prayer, Solomon ben Isaac came over to Judah ben Nathan's house. "I've come to seek shelter in your part of the house," he said, cheerfully, and pinched Elvina's cheek. "Your grandmother has chased me away with her broom, the servants have gone out to draw water, the ground is covered with pots, dishes, and knives, which are about to be dunked in boiling water, and no one has any time to give me a meal!"

Elvina served him a bowl full of piping hot oatmeal and another one to her father, Judah ben Nathan. Samuel and Yom Tov then arrived from the older students' dormitory, where they were now lodging. Yom Tov was sleepily rubbing his eyes.

Judah ben Nathan leaned toward him. "Aren't you feeling well, my son?"

"I dreamed about a dog. It scared me because . . ."

Samuel didn't let him finish his sentence. "Against the sons of Israel not a dog will point his tongue," he recited in a loud voice. Then, turning to his cousin with an air of triumph, he declared, "You have nothing to fear any more because the danger has been cast off."

Solomon ben Isaac smiled. "Excellent. You are as good at explaining away dreams as Meir ben Samuel, your father."

As Elvina placed bowls of oatmeal in front of the boys, she was wondering when she would be able to accomplish the mission she had taken upon herself. To hide how worried she was, she said, "I dreamed I saw a flock of geese. How do you interpret that?"

But Samuel was not to be caught unawares. "I'm surprised you dreamed about geese because the person who dreams about geese may hope to acquire wisdom. As it is written, 'Wisdom declaims in the street,' which is exactly as geese do when they gabble in the courtyards."

"My cousin is most kind." Elvina retorted.

The boys dipped huge pieces of bread in the oatmeal, then sucked on them noisily, as boys do. Wouldn't they ever finish? Mazal, dear Mazal, thought Elvina, don't forget that you have to help me, no obligation, of course, but still, it would be so nice of you to help me take those *matzot* over to Columba's.

"Hurry up," she said. "I have a lot of work to do. I have to make the *haroset.*"

Having his mouth full of oatmeal didn't prevent Samuel from declaring, perfectly seriously, "I'll come supervise you. I seem to remember that last year it was not thick enough."

Elvina nearly choked. "Not thick enough? You, supervise me? Have you gone mad? Who do you think you are?"

Solomon ben Isaac was laughing. "Let him come and watch you, Elvina," he chuckled. "He has everything to learn. It greatly pleases me to see that my grandson Samuel ben Meir, whose head is usually lost somewhere up in the clouds, is concerning himself with the Pesach preparations."

It was wonderful to hear her grandfather laugh—his old carefree laugh from before the events of the previous year. It made Elvina so happy that she almost forgot her mission.

Samuel couldn't get angry, of course, so he sniffled, a little snort of wounded pride. "Are you really in such a hurry?" he asked Elvina. "Don't you want us to recite our Mishnah to you? Usually you're so eager to hear us, so you can show us how much better you pronounce the sacred language than we do."

Elvina bit her lip. She had picked up her distaff and now kept her eyes on the wool passing through her fingers in order to hide her impatience to see them leave. She didn't want to raise any suspicions.

Judah ben Nathan had been eating in silence, deep in his thoughts. He lifted up his head, all of a sudden, and spoke to Solomon ben Isaac. "What do we know about these people, the circumstances of their baptisms? How sincere are they in their repentance? It seems to me we know nothing at all."

Elvina's heart jumped. Her father was talking about Columba's family.

Her grandfather had stopped laughing. "We know that they have chosen to leave the town where they were born, a wealthy household, and several fields in order to begin a new life in a community where they don't know anyone."

Samuel asked, "Have they been observing the Sabbath since their arrival in Troyes?"

Solomon ben Isaac nodded. "I have every reason to think so. And I believe they are preparing for Pesach fittingly."

Elvina was under the impression that her grandfather was looking at her. She felt herself blushing. Could he possibly know something?

Solomon turned to Judah ben Nathan. "These people's lives were threatened," he said quietly. "They felt the knives on their throats. We don't have to receive them with open arms, but let us not be too hard on them. Give them a chance."

"Rabbi Eliezer says that between death and idolatry you must choose death," replied Judah ben Nathan.

Solomon directed toward his son-in-law one of the sharp glances he was famous for, and which could throw off even the bravest of those who dared argue with him. "What about you, my son?" he asked. "Would you suffer martyrdom? Are you quite sure of yourself?"

Judah ben Nathan pinched his lips and tugged at his beard, as he always did when he was displeased. Elvina hated those arguments between them. They were courteous arguments, of course, as was proper between a master and his student, even if the latter had also become a master. But still. She always suffered for her father, who was forced to bow down to the authority of Solomon ben Isaac.

And so she was seized with the desire to restore some kind of balance. She went to sit next to Solomon ben Isaac, and said, amazed that she could be so brazen, "My grandfather knows that my father would suffer a thousand deaths rather than allow himself to be baptized."

Elvina wondered whether she had really dared speak those words or if it had been someone else. But her grandfather smiled at her, and his smile seemed to her to radiate with kindness and tenderness. She didn't dare look at her father. Then, a little abruptly, Solomon ben Isaac pushed back his empty bowl. "I invited them to settle down in

Jeremiah's house because I remembered the decree of our great master Gershom ben Judah, Light of the Exile. Time will tell if I was right. The meal is over. Let us give thanks to Him who gives us our sustenance."

What a relief! Judah ben Nathan, at least, had not guessed her secret. Elvina decided that she would ask her grandfather about Rabbenu Gershom's decree as soon as she had a chance. Meanwhile, she had a delivery to make.

She left the house and ran down the alley to avoid meeting anyone. She reached Forge Street, then the burned house, which was not quite a ruin anymore, since a door and a large window shutter had been installed. Both were made of oak and were thick and strong. And both were tightly closed. Elvina's heart pounded as she put her mouth against the shutter. "Columba," she called in a low voice.

No one. Silence. Could they have moved? People didn't put up a beautiful new door and shutter and then just get up and leave. Elvina was sure that neither Columba nor her mother spent much time at the market. Did they stay locked up in the dark house? Again she called, this time a little louder. "Columba!"

Still no answer. She couldn't just drop the *matzot* on the doorstep. For the third time she called Columba. This time she yelled. A slight scratching sound answered her, like the scratching a mouse makes with its claws. Someone was pushing up a trapdoor that probably led to the cellar. The trapdoor came up just enough to allow Columba to emerge. She immediately bent down and locked it. She was even paler than she had been at the market.

"I called you three times," Elvina said. "What were you doing in your cellar?"

"I went down to draw some wine."

"Here, I brought you some *matzot*," Elvina said.

Columba did not seem surprised. She took the package and slipped it into her sleeve without uttering a word. Then she grabbed both of Elvina's hands and squeezed them, let them go, turned away, quickly opened the door to her house, just a little, and disappeared inside. She never once raised her eyes to look at Elvina's face.

Once again Elvina was running. As she ran, she thanked her *mazal* for keeping away all the gossipy women who would have been delighted to meet her in a place where she had no business at all.

On Market Street, women were bustling around a horseman with a broad, suntanned face. His tunic was dusty and ragged, and he held a huge sack filled with lettuce across his saddle. "Don't fight, ladies!" he joked. "My bag is large. Each and every one of you will get her nice green lettuce, whose bitter taste reminds you of the bitterness of the Jewish people's slavery in Egypt. How do I know that, even though I am not a Jew? Yesterday night I rested for a few hours at an inn. There I met a Jewish merchant, and he explained it all to me. I couldn't understand why I had to gallop like the devil himself, from Rouen to Troyes, loaded with sacks of lettuce. Obviously, after several days on the road, some of the leaves are not so green. But I hurried as fast as I could!"

Had Columba's mother come to buy some lettuce or would she make do with horseradish or other "bitter greens" brought with her among her baggage? Elvina wondered. And what did Columba's mother look like?

And why wasn't Columba holding any kind of jug or pitcher as she came out of the cellar where she had been drawing wine, or so she said, and why were her eyes red, and why did she look so very disheveled?

Chapter
11

*T*he most honorable Lady Angelica asks how to make the haroset *for the Passover seder. A young and humble member of Solomon ben Isaac's family is answering you on his behalf and following his instructions.*

In the house of Solomon of Troyes, I am in charge of preparing the haroset. *I will start as soon as I have finished writing this letter and given it to a merchant who has come to us from Rouen and is about to continue on his way. He is bringing you dates, figs, and spices. But he is completely out of lettuce, not one single little leaf. We, in Troyes, have bought it all! When there is no lettuce, Solomon ben Isaac recommends using horseradish.*

The haroset *represents the mortar with which we made bricks when we were slaves in Egypt. It must be very thick. It is made of dates and dried figs, walnuts and almonds, ginger and cinnamon, and apples. Everything is mixed in wine, which gives it its red color, reminding us of the blood spilled in Egypt. The ginger and cinnamon, because of their rough texture and their color, remind us of the straw the children of Israel used to make the bricks. The apples remind us of the apple trees under which, during the time of their slavery, the daughters of Israel would secretly meet their husbands when the Egyptians imposed upon them harsh separation. They would bring their mirrors and would look at themselves with their husbands and say, "See how pretty I am!" Then they became mothers and gave birth under the very same apple trees, concealed from the eyes of the Egyptians who wanted to kill their babies.*

You dip the bitter greens in the haroset, *then you shake it right off because it tastes good, and you must not sweeten the bitterness of the herbs. But later, during the meal, you can eat it and it is truly delicious!*

Chapter
12

Rachel, my sweet aunt Rachel, I feel like talking to you tonight just as if you were right here next to me. For once, I am not alone. (Old Zipporah snoring in the other bed doesn't count!) Tonight my two cousins Fleurdelys and Hannah are sleeping next to me. We put Hannah in the middle, so she won't fall off the bed.

Fleurdelys is a shy, easily frightened little creature. Before going to bed, she wraps up her curly hair in a scarf. "Don't you cover your head when you sleep?" she asked me, her eyes wide open in amazement.

I laughed. I told her I love to spread and shake my mane on the pillow. Unless it is horribly cold, of course. I assured her that our aunt Rachel often let her hair loose, too, when she used to sleep next to me.

"Don't you know there are mischievous demons who take pleasure in tangling up people's hair while they sleep?" Fleurdelys asked.

I put my finger on her mouth. "Hush, child! We don't speak of these things!"

To bring her mind back to good and pleasant topics, I showed her the notebook on which I copy my favorite psalms. I helped her read the verses we will read on the night of Pesach: "What alarmed you, O sea, that you fled, O Jordan, that you ran backward, O mountains, that you skipped like rams, and you hills, like lambs?"

Fleurdelys gave me that thoughtful look of hers. "I want to start a notebook of my own. This week, will you help me?"

"We can't write during the week of Pesach, but once you get home, I'm sure your mother will be happy to help you. Ask her."

After that, Fleurdelys fell asleep. But then a donkey started to bray, waking up Fleurdelys and also Hannah. Both started sobbing. "Poor little donkey, poor little donkey," Fleurdelys kept repeating. "The Crusaders took him away."

She was thinking about her father's little donkey, which the Crusaders had stolen last year. I reassured her that the donkey we were hearing was the spice merchant's donkey, and that there was no reason to worry. I added that when the donkey brays, you know the first watch of the night is over, and the second is about to begin. Fleurdelys was not convinced. "If there's no reason to worry," she said, "why was Grandmother sobbing and wringing her hands and speaking of danger this afternoon when we arrived?"

"Our grandmother never misses an opportunity to cry and wring her hands," I answered, without a moment's hesitation. "That's the way she is!" (Exactly what you, my dear aunt Rachel, used to say to me not such a long time ago.)

Fleurdelys and Hannah went back to sleep. But soon the convent bells rang matins. My cousins aren't used to this, so they woke up again. I had to explain that there was a convent not far from our house, and that the nuns get up to pray in the middle of the night. A little later some dogs howled, and again my cousins woke up crying. "It's nothing," I told them, "just the second watch coming to an end. The dogs howl—it's a normal thing."

But now Fleurdelys couldn't remember where she was. Our clothes hanging from the bars along the wall seemed to her strange menacing creatures. Zipporah's loud snoring frightened her because she couldn't understand where it came from. So, what did I do? I lifted the canvas from the window, the moonlight filled the room, and everything looked normal again. I said to Fleurdelys and to Hannah, "Look at the moon. She's our friend. She protects us from evildoers by lighting up our town as well as our room with her soft white light. Tomorrow she will be full, but see how beautiful she already is."

That's what you used to say to me when I was afraid and couldn't sleep. My dear, sweet aunt Rachel, now I think I understand why you were never the least bit scared, even when Peter the Hermit's Crusaders invaded our town. You were putting your whole heart into comforting little Elvina. Now, I am holding Hannah in my arms, while stroking Fleurdelys' forehead and hair. I've explained at least ten times that there is nothing to fear and that we can sleep peacefully. Even if there were something to be scared of, I would be too busy to be frightened!

You once said to me, "If the Almighty has made you a girl, He must have had His reasons." Do you suppose one of those reasons might be that I am here, right now, comforting my little cousins, whereas if I were a boy . . .

Let's imagine, dear Aunt Rachel and you, too, dear Mazal, let's imagine . . . What if things were different? Let's imagine Samuel comforting his little sisters, while I would be studying the Talmud . . .

I can just see you yawning, Aunt Rachel. I hear you saying, "Let me get some sleep, Elvina. You make me tired with your upside-down stories."

And you, Mazal, are laughing, of course, laughing at me. You say, "Better make up something else, dear Elvina, because, with the best intentions in the world, I can't follow you there."

Chapter

13

Solomon ben Isaac's house echoed with cries, questions, and orders repeated from person to person.

"Our mistress, there are worms in the lettuce!"

"Wash the leaves one by one!"

"Mistress, we don't have enough bundles of hay!"

"Run to the chicken coop, take some straw, and tie it up with ropes!"

"Mistress Yochebed! The table won't stand up! We need one more trestle!"

"Run and get one in Miriam's house!"

"Zipporah! Our mistress Miriam needs you to bring over the cushions we will lean on!"

"Elvina, go get some nice linen napkins to cover the *matzot*! Make it fast! And while you're at it, bring some dishes; we're running short! Tonight we don't share plates; even the children get plates of their own."

"Do I get a plate all to myself?" Isaac yelled.

"Yes, if you stop jumping around like a puppy."

"Fleurdelys, hold on to your little sister. Don't let her come near the fire."

"Count the number of plates! Don't forget, five of Solomon ben Isaac's students will be with us. Their homes are far away, and they were afraid the roads might be dangerous."

Elvina's grandmother, Precious, who was busily arranging the herbs, the eggs, and the *haroset* on the plates, started to moan and sigh. "Of course they are afraid, poor young men, they have every reason to be afraid. The roads have become so dangerous for us Jews. What about the students who did go home? Shall we ever set eyes on them again? Poor dear boys!"

Fleurdelys nudged Elvina and whispered in her ear. "Look!

Grandmother is about to weep and wring her hands!"

"Remember what I told you," Elvina whispered back. "She never misses an opportunity."

The last few hours before the beginning of Pesach were so frantic that Elvina didn't have a moment to think, not even about the tiny strip of parchment that she had found a little earlier in one of her long, wide sleeves when she pushed them up to work more comfortably. The parchment was rolled up and pressed against the seam so that she hadn't felt it yesterday when she undressed, nor this morning when she dressed. She had just had time to unroll it and see a pretty drawing of a tiny dove, and a few words, written in the sacred language, in a neat and delicate handwriting: "Columba thanks Elvina with all her heart." Elvina had hastily returned the parchment to her sleeve, where it rolled up all by itself, because it had been so tightly rolled before.

The first of their guests had arrived. Old Leah, leaning on her canes, was accompanied by her servant. "Welcome, and be blessed!" Precious called out. "Elvina, help Leah find a place where she can settle down until we start the seder."

Leah had a piercing but sugary sweet voice. "Elvina, dear little Elvina, it so happens I want to speak to you. Where are my *matzot*?"

At first Elvina smiled, then she understood what the question was about, and she blushed. "What *matzot*?" she stammered.

"The *matzot* you were baking at the communal oven, of course! Don't tell me you've already forgotten. The poor sick old woman! Who else could it be but me?"

Leah's eyes were laughing. They were old eyes and nearly blind, but nothing escaped them, especially not the fact that Elvina was embarrassed. Now Elvina remembered how the women had been joking that day. They must have told Leah about the *matzot*. Well, Elvina thought, I'll play her game.

"I don't know what people have been telling you," she answered. "Why don't you taste my *haroset*? Well, what do you think?"

"Delicious, of course, but I want my *matzot*!"

Precious had been listening. "My granddaughter is as red as a beet! You went to the communal oven? What for? Don't we have our own oven?"

Elvina was saved by her mother calling out, "Elvina! Put vinegar cups on the table! Oh, here come Samuel and Yom Tov! Just in time!"

"In time for what? We want some soup. Or vegetables. To stimulate our appetite. This way we will better appreciate the *matzot*, the bread of our affliction."

Elvina burst out laughing. Yochebed stared at Samuel as if she didn't recognize her own son, while she raised both her hands to straighten her headscarf.

"Vegetables? Who has time to serve you vegetables?" she asked. "You'll eat some later. Just bring the chairs, will you? Yom Tov, run to your house to get your father's armchair!"

From another corner of the big room, Miriam was yelling, "Solomon ben Isaac will be here any moment! Quick, somebody place the three *matzot* at the head of the table. And the lettuce! Hurry!"

Everybody was running. Old Leah said, to nobody in particular, "Vinegar, yes, bitter like the tears of our ancestors when they were slaves in Egypt."

Elvina looked at Leah. The sly old woman had forgotten the *matzot*. Finally!

Just then, Isaac, who had been skipping about like a small goat, cried out in his high-pitched voice, "Here comes Grandfather! And Father! And Uncle! And . . . others!"

Solomon was crossing the courtyard. His step was light. Little Isaac ran up to him and grabbed his hand. Solomon stopped on the doorstep.

"What a beautiful table this is," he said. "Are all my grandchildren here?"

Fleurdelys walked up to him, more shyly than her younger brother, then Samuel, and Yom Tov, and Elvina, who was carrying Hannah.

All of a sudden, the room was perfectly silent. Which was astonishing because, just a moment before, the women were all talking at once, Fleurdelys was crying because she had spilled something on her apron, Hannah was crying because she had fallen down, the servants were screaming that they couldn't get all of the worms out of the lettuce and the lettuce from Rouen was never any good, Samuel was complaining that the *haroset* was much too thick and there was no way you could dip the bitter herbs into it, Elvina was replying that it was supposed to be mortar, not soup . . . All this noise and commotion came to a stop the very instant Solomon appeared on the threshold.

Now Precious stood at the head of the table, with Miriam and Yochebed at her sides. Elvina looked at the three of them, her mother, her aunt, her grandmother, starched wimples perfectly in place, brilliantly white holiday headdresses framing their now calm, reassuring faces. Everything was as it should be. The beautiful holiday lamp, Solomon's favorite lamp, made of finely carved silver, was lit and the flame danced.

Just then Elvina remembered Columba. Was her mother at this very moment standing by a pretty lamp brought over from Germany? Were the *matzot* baked by Elvina, Rachel, and Naomi now waiting on a silver plate set in front of Columba's father?

She also thought of Rachel, her sweet aunt Rachel. She was probably sitting down with her mean old husband, who was always threatening to send her home because she wasn't bearing him any children, but never did send her home. Wouldn't she be better off in Troyes among those who loved her?

Solomon looked all around the table, and smiled. "A man who returns from the synagogue, on the eve of a holiday, is accompanied by two angels, a good one and a bad one. When he arrives home and finds the table covered with a nice tablecloth and beautiful settings, the lamps lit and the holiday meal waiting, the good angel speaks to the Almighty and says, 'Grant this man another holiday like this one.' And the bad angel is forced to say, 'Amen.' "

Chapter
14

It was very hot in the room. In previous years, the door and the window had always remained open onto the spring sky, allowing the moonlight to stream in, and to let in any beggar or traveler who happened to walk by. But times had changed. Since the passage of the Crusaders, everyone had become more fearful. Doors were locked, wood shutters closed.

Even like this, Pesach was Elvina's favorite holiday. Each person participated in telling of the suffering of the people of Israel during their slavery and their coming out of Egypt. The children asked questions and received answers. Even Judah ben Nathan seemed happy and relaxed. His lips were not pinched tight, he was not tugging at his beard with the worried, angry look he so often had. Elvina would have liked to hug and kiss them all, her mother, her father, her uncle and her aunt, her grandparents, and even, she really wondered why, Samuel and Yom Tov, who were busy arguing about who would get more cushions to lean on, but she just hugged Fleurdelys, almost choking her with hugs. "What a beautiful feast," she said. "I'm so glad you're here." Timid Fleurdelys shrieked a little, but she was proud and she tried to do everything just like Elvina, this intimidating but so very kind cousin of hers.

Solomon ben Isaac sat at the head of the table, between Isaac and Fleurdelys. "Silence!" he ordered. His voice was strong and joyful. Solomon bent toward Samuel. "Samuel ben Meir, my grandson," he said, "do we lean when we drink the first cup of wine?"

Samuel hesitated. Elvina couldn't believe it. The arrogant Samuel, always so sure of himself, was now being shy.

"Samuel, I'm asking you a question!"

"Yes. We lean in the manner of free men. During the meal, we will tell how we came out of slavery. But women don't lean."

As he said those last words, Samuel shot a glance at Elvina. He was challenging her! Their grandfather now turned to Fleurdelys. His eyes were sparkling. "What do you think? Should the women and the girls also lean?"

Her eyes wide open with panic, Fleurdelys looked at her mother, then at Elvina, as if begging them to come to her help. "Say yes," Elvina whispered in her ear.

"Elvina says yes!"

"Very good! Elvina, explain this."

"Women were slaves in Egypt, just like men. The Almighty performed miracles for them. When they went to draw water from the well . . ." "In order to go wash their husbands' feet in the fields," Yom Tov interrupted her. "Grandfather explained it to us."

But Elvina had made up her mind not be flustered. She looked at Yom Tov and smiled pleasantly before resuming her explanation. "Yes. They drew water and that water was full of little fishes. They fed the fishes to their husbands and said to them, 'Meet us under the apple trees!' Then, some time later, under these same apple trees, they brought forth many children. And so, thanks to the women, the people of Israel survived."

Samuel's fit of shyness had been short-lived. "But women aren't used to leaning," he cried.

"Whereas we all know that you, Samuel, are accustomed to lean when you eat. In fact, you are used to lying down, like the Babylonians."

For a moment, Elvina was afraid she had spoken too sharply. But then she saw that Solomon ben Isaac was thoroughly enjoying himself. The truth was he loved nothing better than listening to his grandchildren argue around the seder table.

Again Samuel challenged Elvina. "The women need to serve the meal. How can they lean?"

Still smiling, Solomon answered him. "In my house, Samuel, the women and the girls lean on cushions because they, too, came out of slavery and became free."

"Do I get to lean on a cushion?" Fleurdelys asked. "Where is my cushion?"

Elvina spoke in her sweetest tone. "Samuel has lots of cushions and he'll give us some, won't you, Samuel?"

At that moment, she noticed that Obadiah did not have a cushion. Solomon had also just noticed. "Obadiah ben Moyses, aren't you going to lean?" he asked.

Obadiah looked at Solomon very earnestly. "Solomon ben Isaac, I am just a student sitting at his master's table."

Obadiah's voice was, as always, calm and serious. But Solomon was smiling and Elvina saw a mischievous twinkle in her grandfather's eye as he answered, "A student, certainly, but it happens that a student could be considered somewhat like a son or grandson. You must lean, my son. Yom Tov, please pass a cushion to your master, Obadiah ben Moyses."

Elvina concentrated on the cup placed in front of her. She hardly noticed when Solomon said the blessing over the first cup of wine, and when everybody drank, she drank, too, without thinking. Nor did she notice when her grandfather pulled the plate of vegetables toward little Isaac, then suddenly pushed it away again, just as Isaac was reaching out to help himself. She didn't see her mother and her aunt pouring the second cup, nor did she see Samuel nudging his younger brother and saying, "Go on! Now's the moment!"

Elvina barely heard Isaac chanting, "Why is this night different from all other nights . . ." She was busy wondering why she felt happy and angry at the same time. Never before had her grandfather said anything that had made her angry. But tonight . . . Obadiah ben Moyses somewhat like a grandson? What was that supposed to mean? A small voice that only Elvina could hear said to her, "Elvina, girl, you're in bad faith. You know the answer perfectly well!" Elvina wasn't convinced. "This is too easy," she replied silently. "In the ballads that my aunt Rachel used to read to me, the noble knight had to accomplish a thousand acts of valor in order to conquer the fair maiden." The voice, as usual, had a ready answer. "You must be dreaming, girl! You are not a fair maiden! Those ballads the Christians write have nothing to do with us. Acts of valor, indeed! Doesn't Obadiah seem noble enough in your eyes when he holds out his hands over the heads of his students, just like Moses, teacher of us all, when he spoke to the children of Israel in the desert? Unless I am very much mistaken, you find him very noble at those times!"

Elvina sighed. She watched her grandfather break one of the

matzot into two pieces and hide one of them under the tablecloth, and she listened to the questions asked by the boys and by Fleurdelys. Then began the retelling of the coming out from Egypt. At the other end of the table, Solomon ben Isaac's students exchanged remarks among themselves, but they became silent whenever Solomon spoke. Elvina's turn came, and she recited, "The Egyptians oppressed the children of Israel with hard labor."

Solomon looked at Fleurdelys and Isaac. "What does that mean?" he asked.

"They had to make bricks," Isaac answered proudly.

"And work in the fields," Fleurdelys added.

Then Samuel said, "The Egyptians forced the men to do women's work and the women to do men's work."

He shot a defiant look at Elvina, as he went on, "The men were the most to be pitied. Men forced to knead dough and bake bread! What a humiliation! And they were clumsy at it because these are not things that come naturally to a man."

Everyone was laughing. They knew how Elvina would react and couldn't wait to hear her. Miriam and Yochebed cheered. "Go on, Elvina! Answer him! Don't let us down!"

Even Judah ben Nathan cried out, "Watch your step, Samuel!"

Elvina could feel Obadiah's eyes resting on her. These eyes were serious and attentive, even though Obadiah was laughing just like the others.

She was about to answer that the women were harassed with work that was much too heavy for them, and that the men's humiliation was nothing compared to the exhaustion of the daughters of Israel, but her words stayed on her lips.

All had heard the gallop of a horse, first far away, then closer and closer, and finally entering the courtyard.

The men had risen from their seats. The women had turned very pale. Yochebed was holding Hannah, while Fleurdelys huddled against Elvina. Their eyes were on the door.

Almost immediately there came several knocks on the thick wood, and a voice, which was not quite the voice of a man, called out, "Please open the door to a friend."

Meir ben Samuel unlocked the door, and in walked a blond boy with very light eyes who was dressed in the manner of a young knight. He seemed embarrassed to find himself the center of attention in a room full of people gaping at him.

Elvina was not the least astonished of them all, but she was the only one who knew the name of the young knight.

"Gauthier," she murmured.

Gauthier saluted her with a little nod, but his eyes settled on Solomon ben Isaac. He walked around the table and bowed deeply in front of him.

Elvina had known this boy when he was filthy, hungry, and hiding in a hole to avoid being sent off to the Crusade. He had lost his mother; he was weeping and wiping off his tears with his mud-covered fists. This new Gauthier was taller and very clean. He wore a tunic of beautiful gray wool and a cloak with a large hood, draped elegantly over his shoulders. The cloak was also gray, its edges adorned with a brightly colored braid of the kind only noblemen were allowed to wear.

The door had been closed again. The men sat down. Solomon looked up coldly at the boy. "I imagine that this young and brilliant knight has a very good reason for honoring us with a visit."

Gauthier bowed again.

"I am not brilliant in any way, Master Solomon. I am just a boy, a student who does not forget his debt toward the family of Solomon of Troyes."

Gauthier's voice had changed, of course. It wasn't as soft as it used to be, but he still expressed himself with that delicacy that appealed so much to Elvina when they used to argue in the dog hole. She was drinking in his words.

"Master Solomon ben Isaac, you are not unaware that this coming week is the Holy Week for the Christians. I have come to warn you that some people in Champagne are talking about imitating those who, in other regions, use this week as a pretext for mistreating Jews. Their goal is to remind the Jews that they hold them responsible for the death of Jesus."

Judah ben Nathan said, "There is no shortage of examples of this. During the Holy Week, the Christians of Béziers throw stones at

Jews with the encouragement of their bishop. In Toulouse, they have the custom of publicly beating a Jew in the city square during that same week."

An appalled silence filled the room. And yet, in spite of the bad news, Elvina was happy. She kissed Fleurdelys. "I was right," she whispered in her ear. "He did not forget me. He really is a friend of the Jews." When she raised her head, she saw Gauthier looking at her. He smiled the proud smile of a boy expecting to be congratulated, as if he were saying to her, "See! I kept my word!"

Elvina returned his smile. Then she saw Obadiah's face. He was not smiling at all. She remembered how violently angry he had been when he learned that she was hiding the fair young Christian with the light eyes.

It was Solomon's turn to bow, very slightly. "We owe our thanks to our young visitor," he said. "Zipporah, give him what he needs to wash his hands, and you, Samuel and Yom Tov, make room for him. Let him eat with us the bread of slavery and poverty, and let him taste with us the wine of freedom."

Chapter

15

Mazal, my dear Mazal, you're making fun of me. I can hear you asking, "Do his eyes still remind you of fresh water? So different from the dark eyes and black beard of Obadiah, which, instead, bring to mind Moses, our master, leading the children of Israel across the desert . . ."

Let me tell you, Mazal, there is not the slightest relation between the two, and you have no business being so sly. Stop laughing! I haven't done anything wrong! I only taught Gauthier to read our sacred language. No, Mazal, you are very wrong, I'm not getting involved in anything at all, just a little lesson this afternoon. Tomorrow he leaves. That's it. You've stopped laughing. Now you're muttering that you're not obliged to fix all of the problems arising from my recklessness, and that one of these days you intend to let me get out of my scrapes on my own, as best I can.

Yesterday evening Gauthier listened respectfully as we recited how the Almighty, with a strong hand, brought us out of our slavery in Egypt. Gauthier never took his eyes off my grandfather. When we drank, he drank, when we recited, he listened so intensely that his brows were knitted, and when we sang, it was obvious that he loved it. He seemed happy and comfortable. He ate the *matzot* with a hearty appetite and watched everything we did as if eager to remember every detail.

After we finished reciting and started serving the meat, the vegetables, and the stewed fruit, conversation became freer. Gauthier turned toward my grandfather and said to him, "Master Solomon ben Isaac, I cannot help noticing that I am being served wine from a separate pitcher."

"It is the tradition," my grandfather replied.

Gauthier was sitting across the table from me, and I could see his face glowing with a sincere desire to learn. "I know," he continued, and his tone was perfectly respectful, "I know, having heard it from the monks, that you avoid drinking wine that we Christians have touched. The point is to avoid touching wine that might have been used to make pagan libations, isn't it?"

"Our young guest is well informed," said my grandfather. "I hope he doesn't take this as a personal insult. We do not for a moment suspect our Christian neighbors and friends of using wine for the cult of pagan gods. However, we prefer to maintain the tradition."

Gauthier bowed his head a little.

Just at this moment, there was another knock at the door. Women's voices were calling out, "Quick! Open up!"

My uncle opened the door and in rushed the two women servants of Nathan ben Simon and Joseph ben Simon, Muriel's father. Both were wrapped from head to toe in their cloaks. In spite of the full moon, they carried torches and were trembling with fear. As they came in, we all caught a glimpse of Gauthier's horse. We had forgotten the horse! It was a magnificent horse, whose shiny coat seemed to attract the moonlight.

I guess my grandfather, too, had forgotten the horse's existence. When he saw him, he seemed startled, but then he immediately said, "This animal cannot remain in our courtyard!"

"My horse will not cause any damage, I assure you," said Gauthier.

"It's not that."

My grandfather's eyes were on the open door and on the horse. "This horse must be sheltered," he repeated.

I shivered with horror. My grandfather was thinking of the cat.

"After dinner, we'll walk the horse over to Simonet's, or to Dieule-sault's," my uncle Meir said.

During that time, the two servants were explaining the purpose of their visit. "Mistress Precious, Mistress Miriam, please come over, quick! Please come and take care of little Toby!"

My mother had risen from her seat. "What's the matter?"

"The poor child is coughing so, it breaks your heart. And he has a fever."

My grandfather answered, "Go home and tell your mistress they will come as soon as we have finished."

The two women looked uncertain. "We hoped they would come back with us. The streets are deserted."

This time my grandfather's tone did not allow for any reply. "Go home. We'll soon be finished and then they will come over."

They left. Our holiday meal ended less joyfully than it should have.

Solomon ben Isaac was preoccupied. Miriam and Precious were discussing medicines and potions. Fleurdelys and Isaac were fast asleep, their heads on the table. My aunt Yochebed couldn't take her worried eyes off them and kept repeating, "I hope they're not coming down with something. God forbid they should be ill!"

"They're just tired," my mother answered. "You'll rub them with rose oil before putting them to bed. Don't you remember how we always used to fall asleep during holiday dinners?"

Out in the courtyard, the horse was whinnying. I could see that Gauthier was dying to go out and take care of him, but he didn't dare leave the table. Samuel and Yom Tov had become restless. I think they, too, were itching to go out and see the horse. Obadiah had launched into some kind of discussion with the other students and didn't look at me again.

Finally my grandfather distributed the pieces of the *afikoman*, the part of the matzah that he had hidden under the tablecloth. We all ate without paying much attention, but my grandfather actually took his piece and forgot to eat it. My father was the one who pointed it out to him. We had already recited the blessing and drunk the third cup of wine. Samuel shook himself out of his stupor and asked Solomon ben Isaac, "What will my grandfather decide? Should we recite the blessing again? Do we drink the third cup again? The *afikoman* represents the paschal sacrifice at the time of the Temple."

I have to hand it to my cousin. He is admirable! One day he will have many students, I'm sure, but I really feel sorry for them. Yes, I feel very sorry for my cousin's future household!

My grandfather seemed annoyed. This had never happened to him! For a brief moment the conversations stopped. We were all wondering what his decision would be. But he just said that he had obeyed the commandment of eating the *matzot* during the meal, that it was late, that it was time to finish and put the children to bed.

My mother and my grandmother filled their baskets with potions and medicines, and my father escorted them to Nathan ben Simon's house. My uncle and Obadiah walked the horse to Dieulesault's, and the boys took Gauthier with them to sleep in the students' dormitory.

That was yesterday, my dear Mazal. Today is different, as you already know, I'm sure.

Chapter

16

Today, Mazal, Toby is very sick. My mother and grandmother stayed the night with him and then my grandmother came home. She entered our house and announced in a very loud voice, "The child is perfectly healthy!" Then she dropped onto a bench. Her clothes and headscarf smelled of the sandalwood that is burned next to a sick person's bed in order to purify the air. "At dawn, the fever was refusing to go down," she explained. "So they decided to change his name."

My heart missed a beat. If they're changing his name, to prevent the Angel of Death from finding him, that means things are very bad. My grandmother was now speaking in a very low voice.

"The child's parents are in a state of panic," she whispered. "The mother is sure that this sickness was wished on the child by her sister, who, having no child of her own, is very jealous of her. She told me that every time she sees her sister, she feels her jealousy like a knife aimed at her little boy. Nathan ben Simon has not left his child's bedside. He has spent the whole night reciting every prayer he knows and all of the verses that Obadiah copied on Toby's wax tablet. Every time the boy opened his eyes, he made him repeat words, hoping that the evil spirits would not dare attack a person who was studying the Torah. Unfortunately, the harm was already done, they had already attacked."

I thought of little Toby, pink, round-cheeked little Toby, carefully reciting his lesson just a few days ago.

"What does Grandfather say about the change of name?" I asked.

My grandmother shrugged her shoulders. "You know your grandfather. The less you mention that kind of topic to him the better."

"For a name change, you need ten men," I said. "And the new name has to be officially inscribed on a parchment."

"Your uncle Meir is taking care of it. He read the formula that makes a new person out of Toby, a new person who has just been born and will enjoy a long life. Nathan had called in all the neighbors."

"What name did they choose?"

"David, of course. Like the King of Israel."

"They couldn't do better. So now Toby has become David."

My grandmother stroked my hair and sighed an exhausted sigh. "I'm too old to stay up all night by a sick child. Make me a cup of herb tea, then I'll go sleep. I'm so glad tonight's meal will be taking place at your house."

I kissed my little grandmother, who has become rather small lately, and whose cheeks look all crumpled, like apples that have spent the winter in the cellar. I prepared some really good fennel tea for her. My aunt Yochebed came downstairs. Her children were still asleep. She pinched both of my cheeks, smoothed my braids, looked at me hard and long, then kissed me and said, "Our Elvina is growing uglier by the day!"

The remark seemed to perk up my grandmother, who began to laugh. "Yes, she is very plain, and you never have to tell her twice to polish the silver Sabbath plate! She wouldn't want to miss a chance to admire herself in it!"

"My grandmother is mistaken!" I cried.

I've always thought that my grandmother had several pairs of eyes. She knows absolutely everything! I can't deny that I rather enjoy looking at myself, just to see what others see when they look at me. But I don't do it very often. And I would hate people to think I'm vain.

My grandmother seemed to be having fun; even her eyes were laughing. "Don't protest, child! You're neither the first, nor the last! Ask your aunt!"

My aunt Yochebed was also laughing. "Our little Elvina needs a mirror, her own mirror!"

But what she gave to me wasn't a mirror. She took a small, clean, and very tightly rolled parchment from her sleeve and tied it around my neck with a string.

"What verse are you giving me?" I asked.

"'The Lord is my shepherd, I shall not want.' Your uncle Meir inscribed it. He inscribed several for me before we left home the other day. You can imagine, when I travel with the children . . ."

Yes, she would want them to be protected by the verses.

My grandmother and my aunt left the room together. My aunt was going to take several medicines to my mother for Toby—I mean David.

A little later, Samuel, Yom Tov, and Gauthier arrived. I saw them crossing the courtyard; they looked alike, three boys who had just woken up and were hungry. The only difference was that Gauthier said good morning to me very graciously, while my brother and my cousin let out their usual grunts, which mean, "Serve us our oatmeal, girl, and hurry up!" Except, of course, that during the Pesach week there is no oatmeal. Zipporah had boiled some eggs, which they ate with *matzot*. Yom Tov explained to Gauthier that boiled eggs improve your memory.

Samuel made a face. "That's common knowledge. Don't bore our guest with things everybody knows."

But Gauthier smiled to Yom Tov, as you smile to a little brother who has just told you something interesting. "I didn't know eggs had that property," he said. "You Jews find in your books all sorts of things that we don't know. So, Yom Tov, I thank you."

Such politeness! Here he was, thanking Yom Tov. Samuel shrugged his shoulders. Their eyes were puffy; they had spent half the night arguing. Gauthier loves a good discussion, and Samuel enjoys flaunting his knowledge and rubbing his ideas against other people's. I have to admit that Samuel knows by heart almost the entire Bible in the sacred language! Gauthier knows the Latin translation. The two of them picked up their discussion where they had left it and started arguing about vocabulary.

I sat down at the table to listen to them while eating my eggs. I was mostly interested in hearing Gauthier. What Samuel says, I usually already know, even if I don't have the time to learn everything by heart the way he does. What Gauthier was saying was new to me. He began by announcing that he wanted to study our sacred language.

"My teachers can't read it. But a monk who has come from another monastery talked to us last week about the mistakes in the Latin translation. He thinks Christians should learn to read the language of the Jews."

I'm pretty sure I was gaping at him. Then I glanced at Samuel. He was trying to look as if he had always known this. But he was just as surprised as I was.

"Would you like me to give you an example?" Gauthier asked, looking at me. I nodded.

"Do you remember Jacob's blessings to his sons?"

"Of course."

"Do you remember what he says to Judah?"

"Yes."

"I know these verses by heart!" Yom Tov yelled. "Obadiah made us learn them last year."

Gauthier smiled at him again. "Recite them. But you'll have to translate them for me."

Proudly, Yom Tov stood up and recited, first in the sacred language, then in our French everyday language. "He binds his foal to the vine and his donkey's colt to a choice vine . . ."

"Go on!" urged Gauthier.

Yom Tov recited up to "His eyes will be as dark as wine, his teeth whiter than milk."

Gauthier had listened attentively. "You'll be surprised to hear that our Latin translation, which is Saint Jerome's, says, 'His eyes are more beautiful than wine.' Obviously it is a mistake."

Samuel banged on the table with his fist, several times, as men do when they are having a discussion. "More beautiful than wine! More beautiful than wine! This doesn't mean anything! If you drink too much wine, your eyes are red, everybody knows that!"

I looked at Gauthier, worried that he might be finding my cousin ridiculous. But no. He was just as absorbed by the discussion as Samuel was.

"Precisely," he replied. "And I know that Solomon ben Isaac, in his commentary, has explained your translation, which is the correct one. That is why I wish to learn your sacred language."

Samuel and Yom Tov got up to go off to the synagogue. Gauthier was surprised. "You study even on a holiday?"

"We read passages of the Talmud relating to the Passover, and we listen to our masters commenting on these passages. But we don't write."

Yom Tov had been looking out of the window and observing the sky. "If the weather is nice, Solomon ben Isaac will take us for a walk. I think we'll go see Baruch, who raises bees. My grandfather loves honey!"

Gauthier got up to say good-bye. He hesitated for a moment, then he said to Samuel, "Listen. I have a request to present to Master Solomon ben Isaac, but I don't dare present it myself."

Samuel was frowning and making himself look important. I hate it when he does that, but Gauthier wasn't put off. "I would like to see Master

Solomon's drawings, especially his map of the Holy Land . . ."

Samuel interrupted him, "Where you didn't go."

"Thanks to Elvina." Gauthier bowed in my direction.

I looked at him, at his light eyes, yes, just like fresh water, and I remembered how I had found him crouching in his muddy hole, and how scared I was that someone would see me bringing him food, and now, here he was, having breakfast with my brother and my cousin, discussing problems of translation. And so, to hide the fact that I was not entirely pleased with this new situation, I started to laugh. And Gauthier laughed. And Yom Tov laughed. Even Samuel began to laugh, and then we couldn't stop laughing, and the whole house echoed with our peals of laughter. You, too, Mazal, must have had a good laugh!

The first to get a grip on himself was, of course, Samuel. He seemed surprised to have let himself go that way, especially in the company of a Christian. He smoothed his tunic with both hands, as if he expected to find some crumbs of laughter still clinging to the material. Then he draped himself in his cloak and even put on his hood in his effort to look dignified.

We had not heard the children coming down. Fleurdelys was carrying Hannah in her arms. They were hungry. I told Zipporah to prepare something for them to eat.

Samuel promised Gauthier they would look at the drawings together, tomorrow, before Gauthier had to be on his way. He added, proudly, "I know these drawings better than most people, because more than once my grandfather has asked me to copy them to illustrate passages from his commentary to send to his correspondents. My father and my uncle make beautiful copies of his commentary, but I'm better at drawing than any of them."

Gauthier looked very impressed, which went straight to my cousin's heart. Finally Yom Tov and Samuel left. Gauthier asked me if I could teach him to read our sacred characters right away. I went upstairs to my chest and found the pieces of parchment I used last year to teach Naomi and Rachel.

We sat down at the table, and even before the children started to eat, he already could recognize many of the characters. Isaac corrected him when he made mistakes, and Gauthier thanked him very politely. Isaac was bursting with pride. Then Gauthier announced he was going to study by the riverside. He caught me by my sleeve, as he used to do last year. "This promises to be a beautiful day. Come join me. You can go on teaching me there. I'm a good student, don't you think?"

He had that mischievous look he sometimes had last year, in his hole. "You don't have to hide onions or cheese in your sleeves for me any more," he teased.

And then I actually heard myself answering, "Yes, I'll come as soon as I can."

Suddenly I didn't feel so comfortable and self-assured anymore. I could hear you, Mazal. You were laughing at me and saying, "A date! What was I telling you? Are you happy now?"

So, very quickly, I added, "Today is a holiday. I'll take Fleurdelys for a walk by the river."

My aunt Yochebed returned just as Gauthier was leaving. She eyed him suspiciously but didn't say anything. She rushed to her children. "Give me your hands, stick out your tongues, you're not feeling feverish, are you, you're not sweating? Are you wearing your amulets? Are you eating? Didn't Elvina make you wash your hands? Zipporah, bring some hot water!"

She began to wash all of their hands, washing each hand at least three times. She seemed really in a panic. "Why didn't you ask Zipporah for hot water? Fleurdelys, what were you thinking about? Can't I turn my back away for one single moment?"

"It's because of Shibbeta, you know," Fleurdelys whispered in my ear. "He attacks children who don't wash their hands before eating. He hides in their food and then attacks them. He gives them sore throats and makes them cough, and sometimes chokes them to death!"

She was speaking louder and louder, and her father, who had just entered the room, overheard the last words. "Who is speaking about Shibbeta? Haven't I explained to you that Shibbeta is a very old demon who does not haunt our regions?"

Meir ben Samuel's face was serene.

"Well, how is the child?" Aunt Yochebed asked him.

"Healthy, perfectly healthy," was the answer.

Uncle Meir rested his hands for a moment on his children's heads, and also on mine. Then he sat down next to us. While my aunt was washing his hands, he said, "Last night I dreamed I was walking in the middle of a large olive grove."

My aunt Yochebed burst out laughing. "How did you know it was an olive grove? You've never seen an olive tree. They don't grow anywhere around here."

"In my dream, I knew perfectly well that they were olive trees, beautiful trees, heavy with olives. And I woke up reciting . . . reciting what?" He turned to his children, who were silently and adoringly staring at him.

He gave the answer himself. "Reciting the verse, 'Your children are like olive plants around your table.' Then I come back here and I find you all sitting around the table! Blessed be the Almighty!"

I often think that my uncle Meir is different from other men and that my aunt Yochebed is very lucky. But it doesn't seem to prevent her from worrying all the time.

Chapter

17

The river bank smelled lovely. Bright little tufts of new grass were growing among the old grass, turned yellow by the winter frosts. There were
daisies everywhere. The apple trees were in full bloom, as were the
blackthorns, with their tiny white flowers.

Elvina and Fleurdelys walked toward the brown peaceful water,
on the surface of which thousands of little lights were dancing. Elvina
had not told her cousin the real purpose of this outing. She wondered
where Gauthier was hiding.

The sound of a flute reached their ears. Elvina stopped to listen.
It was a tune she had never heard before, with a refrain that kept coming back, and, each time, ended on a long note that gripped her heart
and left her a little sad, but it was so beautiful that she wanted it to last
and last. She was so absorbed, she didn't notice that Fleurdelys had left
her side to go smell the flowers on the bushes.

A wild neighing roused her. A horseman had been riding toward
the river to allow his horse to drink, but Elvina hadn't seen him. Suddenly, right in front of her, the horse reared and the horseman yelled
something in Elvina's direction, but she couldn't hear him because of
the horse's neighing. The horse calmed down, but refused to move forward. This time Elvina heard the horseman yelling, "You dirty little Jew-
ess! You've cast a spell on my horse!"

He brandished his horsewhip as if to hit Elvina, who stood stock-
still, rooted to her place, dying of fear, her eyes on the whip. It didn't
occur to her to move back or run away.

"Watch out, you Jew girl!" the horseman was saying. "If you
don't undo your spell right away, you'll be sorry!"

"This young lady has most certainly not cast a spell on your
horse. She is the granddaughter of Master Solomon ben Isaac of Troyes,
of great repute."

Gauthier! In one hand he held his flute and also Elvina's tablets and parchments. With his other hand he calmly patted the horse's nose.

"I don't know you, boy," grumbled the horseman, "but you seem all right."

Gauthier used his flute to point to the grass. "I've seen several snakes warming themselves in the sun. I imagine that's what scared your horse."

Elvina still couldn't move. Her heart was beating so fast it hurt. Never in her entire life had she been so scared! Never in her entire life had anyone hit her or even threatened to hit her! With a horsewhip!

All of a sudden, familiar voices surrounded her. "Elvina! What's happening? Your cousin Fleurdelys called us to the rescue! She was sobbing that you were in danger, that you were being accused of witchcraft . . . We were washing clothes in the river, so we rushed up!"

Jeanne and Marguerite were the daughters of Master Hubert, a Christian farmer with whom Solomon ben Isaac was on friendly terms. They now stood on either side of Elvina and held her hands. Little by little, Elvina's heart returned to its normal beat. But her throat was so knotted she couldn't utter a word. Fleurdelys stood very close to her, crying and hiccupping.

The horseman looked down at all of them. Marguerite, who was the eldest of the sisters, spoke up to him. "This is our friend. Her family is very respected in our town."

"All right, that's enough," the horseman said. "I'll take my horse to drink and get out of here before the whole town gathers to defend this girl."

"The honorable thing would be to apologize to her." As he spoke, Gauthier smiled. He looked so handsome, so well-mannered that the horseman couldn't help smiling, too. He turned toward Elvina. "Please, girl, forgive me. I made a mistake. And now, if you will all kindly give me your permission, I'll be on my way."

Marguerite and Jeanne laughed as they kissed Elvina. "To be rescued by such a handsome young man," they teased her. "Lucky Elvina!"

Gauthier had turned his back and pretended not to hear. By now, Elvina had recovered. She was calm enough to see that Gauthier wasn't taking any notice of Marguerite and Jeanne, although they were

Christians, just like him. And, in her heart of hearts, Elvina was rather pleased.

Jeanne watched the horseman as he rode away. "What did you do to him?" she asked Elvina in a matter-of fact tone. "Fleurdelys was too upset to give us an explanation."

Again Elvina's heart started pounding. She tore her hands out of Marguerite's and Jeanne's hands, stepped away from them, and screamed, "I didn't do anything to him! What are you thinking? What could I possibly do to a horseman sitting on his horse?"

Fleurdelys burst into tears again.

"Don't cry, Fleurdelys, we don't wish your cousin any harm." Marguerite stroked her cheek. Then she turned to Elvina. "I have to tell you, something horrible happened, this morning. One of our geese . . ."

"Our geese that you hate. You're always saying they're worse than dogs," interrupted Jeanne.

"Somebody slit her throat," Marguerite continued. "We found her in our courtyard this morning. The head was detached from the body. Who could have done such a thing?"

Elvina immediately thought of the cat. Marguerite was observing her. "You look like you know something," she said.

Elvina remembered her grandfather's words. He had forbidden her to mention the slaughtered cat. "No, I don't know anything," she replied.

But Marguerite was shaking her head. "That's what you say. Anyway, we have to return to our laundry. The days are still short."

She had grabbed her sister's arm. Elvina watched them as they walked off together. Even their backs seemed angry. Elvina couldn't stand it. She was aching all over as if she had been beaten for real, she had been horribly frightened, and now, on top of that, her friends were angry at her. "I'm sorry about your goose!" she yelled. "If I hear something, I'll let you know."

The two didn't even turn around and Elvina thought she saw Marguerite shrugging her shoulders. But Fleurdelys had slipped her small hand into Elvina's, and Gauthier was standing near her. "Let them go," he said. "You'd do much better to come and help me read these verses."

Chapter

18

$\mathcal{M}$azal, my dear Mazal, I'm sure you were watching over me this afternoon, and I owe you a thousand thanks. Never in my entire life have I been so frightened. Would this man really have beaten me if Gauthier hadn't intervened? Mazal, please don't be smug, don't tell me it was my fault! You're not saying anything? Good!

After that terrifying event, we sat down by the water. Gauthier had found a really nice place under a tree. I can't believe how easily he is learning to read our sacred language. We started out by reading the first verses of the Bible, "*Bereshit bara Elohim . . .*" and translating, "When God began to create heaven and earth—the earth being *tohu* and *bohu*," as I did with Naomi and Rachel last year. Gauthier knows the verses by heart in Latin, so he had no difficulty remembering the words in the sacred language.

Each time he made a mistake Fleurdelys would burst out laughing and hide her face against my shoulder. Then Gauthier would look miffed. "You'll see, little Fleurdelys," he said, "soon I'll be reading as well as your big brother and your cousin Yom Tov."

"You mean, 'as well as you and your cousin Elvina,'" I corrected him.

Gauthier bowed respectfully, but his eyes were laughing. "Yes, you're right, of course, that's what I meant!"

I told him exactly what I used to tell Naomi and Rachel, that you must read each passage over and over again, more than a hundred times, until you read it perfectly. I told him what Obadiah repeats every single day to his students that you must neither stutter nor stumble. I explained *tohu* and *bohu* to him, the way my grandfather does. I taught him that *tohu* means "astonishment and amazement" and *bohu* "emptiness and solitude."

My student's eyes were shining with pleasure. "Is that the explanation given by Master Solomon ben Isaac?"

"Yes. Does it surprise you?"

"It doesn't surprise me, but I am so happy to learn the explanations of such a master. It's a great honor."

Then, a little sadly, he sighed. "Maybe some day Solomon ben Isaac will allow me to come and sit at his feet and learn from him even though I am not Jewish! But I think he distrusts me."

"He doesn't distrust you, personally," I answered. "You must understand that we are living in difficult times."

Gauthier was silent for a moment, then he asked, "Do you think he will agree to show me his drawings of the Holy Land?"

"Samuel promised you he would, didn't he?"

"Have you seen them?" Gauthier asked me.

"Of course. More than once. When I was little, I used to climb up on my grandfather's lap, and he showed them to me. I sometimes even watched him draw."

"How lucky you are! Describe the drawings of the Holy Land."

"But you're going to see them."

"Describe them anyway. It will help me understand them better."

"My grandfather says that these drawings are not his drawings, that all he had to do was follow the instructions given to Moses by the Almighty, when He says, 'This is the land that will fall to you as your inheritance, the land of Canaan with its boundaries.' The Almighty says: you will draw a line here, and another line there, here there will be a border going from the mountain to the sea, and there a border going from the mountain to the river. That's why my grandfather modestly assures us that all he had to do was hold the quill. But it is not given to everyone to hold the quill as well as Solomon ben Isaac holds it."

Fleurdelys was leaning over the edge of the river, admiring her reflection in the water. "Elvina!" she called. "I can see my whole face and my hair! And the top of my dress! This is much better than my mother's mirror, where I can barely see the tip of my nose!"

But then she ran back to me and reminded me that we were supposed to set the table for the second holiday meal, which was taking place in our house. Gauthier said he was really looking forward to it. "Tomorrow I shall return to the monastery where I study. I have one more favor to ask from you. I'd like to continue to make progress in reading your sacred language. Do you have other parchments to lend me, with other verses? And also some models so I can learn to write the letters?"

I had already given him all the parchments I had been keeping in my trunk. I told him I would find him some other parchments, but not if he left at dawn, because I could only get them in the morning. The only person I could ask for parchments was Obadiah.

Gauthier smiled and looked surprised. "You intend to ask Obadiah? I don't think he'll be thrilled. My presence irritates him and he can't wait to see me return to where I came from!"

Still smiling, Gauthier looked at me for a moment, then added, "If I were in his place, I believe I would be in exactly the same frame of mind."

I pretended not to hear. Fleurdelys was tugging at my sleeve. "Come! It is past midday. Grandmother will be worried!"

Gauthier had once more settled down under his tree and was bending over his parchments.

Before leaving him, I said, "I often heard my grandfather say that it is good to study next to a river, because just as the river flows from its source, so knowledge will flow from your mouth."

Gauthier raised up his eyes to me. "What a beautiful thought," he said seriously. "I will not forget it."

Chapter
19

Elvina gently closed the door of the school, slid into what she thought of as "her" vestibule, and sat down on "her" stool. The semi-darkness was restful, even if, just a few feet away, the boys were reciting their lessons at the top of their lungs while swaying back and forth over the sheets of parchment on which their master had copied the passages they had to learn. The wax tablets had been put away in the school chest, since writing is to be avoided during the Passover week.

Elvina could hear Obadiah's voice above the voices of the older boys. He was reading very slowly with the younger pupils. Today, her cousin Isaac was sitting with them. There was no reason for him to stay at home doing nothing and not learning, even if he was only visiting for a week.

Elvina particularly enjoyed listening to Obadiah when he was teaching the younger boys, those who had recently started school. She admired the infinite patience with which he articulated each word so that they could repeat it after him, and also the way he pronounced and chanted the words of the sacred language.

Obadiah read, then translated, "For the land that you are about to enter and possess is not like the land of Egypt from which you have come. There the grain you sowed had to be watered by your foot, like a vegetable garden."

Then he read again and the little boys repeated after him.

When Obadiah picked up his stick and twirled it above the boys' heads the room became absolutely quiet. It's a miracle, thought Elvina. He never needs to hit or even threaten a student, as other schoolmasters do. Obadiah raises his stick in the air, and all of the boys calm down.

"Can someone explain 'watered by your foot'?" Obadiah asked.

The boys were throwing sidelong glances at each other; some were hiding under their hoods.

"Watered by your foot," Obadiah repeated. "Think. Your parents have vegetable gardens. How do they water them?"

"Not with their feet!" Several boys laughed.

At that moment, Elvina heard a strange noise, a kind of rubbing, or scratching, coming from a dark corner of her vestibule not far from her. She stood up and wrapped herself tightly in her cloak. Could it be a rat? She hated rats! She could make out a form crouching in the corner, something she had not noticed, something much bigger than a rat. A cat? A fox? Suddenly it sprang forward. Elvina let out a scream and flattened herself against the wall. A young boy brushed past her, stumbled on the stool, regained his balance, and, raising his hand, called out, "Watered with your foot means walking and carrying buckets in order to water places where there is no water."

He caught his breath and chanted, in the sacred language, "You watered by your foot, like a vegetable garden." He had lowered his voice but his pronunciation was perfect. After that, as if terrified by his own rashness, he covered his mouth with both hands and stood there, facing the class, petrified.

The whole class had turned around all at once. Those who were dozing had awakened and pushed back their hoods, and all were gaping at the scrawny boy with rumpled blond hair who had sprung out of the wall for the sole purpose of chanting a verse in his clear high-pitched voice.

Obadiah was no less flabbergasted than his students. Now that she had recovered from her fright, Elvina could hardly keep from laughing out loud. This boy had to be Columba's little brother! How learned he was for such a small child!

Obadiah walked over to the boy. "Why are you hiding? Come and sit with the others. What's your name?"

The child was not so self-assured anymore, and he answered in a small voice that sounded very much like Columba's. "My name is Godolias."

"Godolias. Come and sit here. Jacquet will share his blanket with you; it's wide enough for two."

From where she stood, Elvina could see Jacquet wriggling a little, without really making any room. The boys were openly whispering to each other. Obadiah motioned to the newcomer to walk up. One boy stretched out his leg. Godolias tripped and fell. All the boys laughed, then another boy pushed him as he was trying to get back on his feet. This time he remained where he was, crouching against the wall. The classroom was buzzing, but not with the words of the sacred text.

"Silence!" Obadiah's voice rang out. "I believe I told you to make room for the new student."

"Not next to me!"

"Not next to me, either!"

One of the older boys got up. "Master, we know who this boy is. Even though this is the first time we have seen him, we know."

"What do you know?"

"That he and his family are people who have been made unclean by the waters of baptism. They are no longer Jews."

"Who says they are no longer Jews?"

"My father says so!" A tall sturdy boy cried out and cast a look of triumph all around him.

Elvina held her breath. What was Obadiah going to do? She didn't have to wait long for the answer. Obadiah had helped Godolias to his feet. He kept his hands, protectively, on the shoulders of the boy, who was shaking with terror.

Then Obadiah spoke. He did not raise his voice, but he hammered out every syllable. "If Master Solomon ben Isaac allowed this boy's parents to settle in our community, if he considers them to be sincere in their repenting, if he did not chase away Godolias's father when he came to the synagogue for the Sabbath prayer, is it for you to refuse to welcome Godolias in this school? Do you have the right to question Master Solomon ben Isaac's decision on this matter? What do you think? Answer me."

The tall sturdy boy, who seemed so proud a few moments ago, was sitting down and examining his fingernails with the utmost concentration. The other boys were silent. You could hear the birds chirping outside.

"Do you remember," Obadiah went on, "do you remember how scared we all were last year when the Crusaders invaded our region and were walking up and down our streets, stealing chickens and sheep? What did we do?"

"We locked ourselves up in our houses."

"Yes. And what if, instead of being satisfied with taking chickens and sheep, they had grabbed one of you with one hand and held a dagger or a sword in the other, and had said, 'Submit to baptism or I will cut your throat!' What would you have chosen?"

"To be slaughtered!"

"To have my throat slit!"

"To die, of course!"

Obadiah smiled the same sad smile Elvina had so often seen on her grandfather's face this past year.

"What makes you so sure?" he asked. "Martyrdom, to sanctify God's Name, is a beautiful thing, but not everyone is capable of it. You have no right to judge Godolias and his family. Give thanks to the Almighty, who has spared you such a test. You are now going to make room for Godolias. You will allow him to sit down, and you will welcome him in our town of Troyes, where he is a stranger. And you will all repeat this verse after me until you know it by heart. 'You shall not wrong a stranger or oppress him, for you were strangers in the land of Egypt.'"

Elvina was happy to see her cousin Isaac inviting Godolias to come and sit next to him, and smiling at him when he did so.

Soon it would be recess time, and that's when she intended to ask Obadiah for some parchments to give to Gauthier. Elvina's heart began to beat a little faster.

Chapter

20

In the schoolyard the boys chased each other or played ball. Three older students had gathered around their master and were asking him questions. Isaac and Godolias stood together in a corner of the yard, watching the other boys play. The weather was mild. A few large drops of rain had fallen earlier, awakening the frogs in a nearby pond. Now they were croaking as loudly as they could, showing that they, too, were coming out of their long winter sleep.

Gathering her courage, Elvina walked up to Obadiah and asked, in a tone that she hoped was light and matter-of-fact, "I wonder if I could have a few parchments with Bible verses copied on them, like those you give to the younger pupils."

The three boys who were with Obadiah had immediately moved away to show their discretion. They pretended to speak among themselves, but Elvina was sure they were listening to every word she and Obadiah uttered.

"You want reading material for your cousin Isaac?" Obadiah asked. "He's a very nice boy, and I congratulate you, but if you want to teach him, it seems to me you have everything you need in your grandfather's house."

"It's not for Isaac."

"Well then, I don't see . . ."

He had to be doing it on purpose, Elvina thought. He knew exactly why she was asking, but he wanted to force her to say it. All right, she would say it.

"It's for Gauthier."

She said it so loud that the three boys swung around. Elvina saw them nudging each other: what fun it would be to witness a quarrel between their schoolmaster and the granddaughter of Solomon ben Isaac.

"Ha!" Obadiah looked like he might spit. "Your little Crusader!"

"He's not a Crusader, he's not mine, and he's not that little!"

As she spoke those last words, Elvina threw a mischievous glance at Obadiah. But Obadiah's eyes were closely following the ball that a boy had thrown high up in the air.

"Crusader or not," Obadiah replied, "he's a liar. The Jews of Troyes have not been in the slightest danger since the Crusaders left."

"What about the cat?" Elvina whispered. "Slaughtered in our very courtyard! On the Sabbath! I know my grandfather told you about it."

Obadiah shrugged his shoulders. "A disagreeable event, of course, but one day we'll find out who did it. Our Christian neighbors are our friends, and your Gauthier . . ."

"He is not *my* Gauthier!"

". . . just wanted a pretext to come and see what the Pesach holiday was like in the house of Solomon ben Isaac."

"What harm is there in that?"

Obadiah didn't answer her question but continued on his own train of thought. "He made up this story to find favor in your grandfather's eyes. He just wanted to see you again."

"He intends to study our sacred language in order to read the Bible. He explained to us that there are mistakes in the Latin translation. Ask Samuel!"

"You expect me to believe that such a pretty little knight has taken it upon himself to correct the mistakes in the Latin Bible?"

"I, for one, believe it. Samuel believes it, too."

"The two of you are nothing but children."

All of a sudden Obadiah's face broke into a smile. "Never before have I heard the daughter of my master Judah ben Nathan invoking the authority of her cousin Samuel ben Meir!"

Elvina bit her lip. She kept her eyes glued on Isaac and Godolias, as if the two little boys were doing something really remarkable. There was no way she would look at Obadiah and see him enjoying his little victory. She kept silent.

"So you want some of the pages I copied for my pupils?" Obadiah asked.

"I would not normally have disturbed you, but you know we

don't write during the week of Passover unless it is absolutely necessary," Elvina answered in a most conciliatory, reasonable tone.

"And this is not absolutely necessary?"

Elvina could hear the laughter in Obadiah's voice. She hesitated
but then looked up at him. Indeed, he was laughing in his beard. She did
not want to laugh, but she smiled and shook her head. "No, it's not."

Obadiah whistled, clapped his hands, and called out the boys'
names. Recess was over. He told Elvina to follow him. "I happen to have
several parchments with nicely copied passages. They're in the school
chest. I'll give them to you."

While the boys settled down again in the classroom, Obadiah
searched in the chest. He handed her several sheets of parchment.
"Here, choose the ones you want."

Elvina examined the parchments, and while she was doing so,
she said, "Gauthier has heard of my grandfather's drawings and asked
to see them. Samuel and I showed them to him earlier today. He actually told Samuel that he would give a lot to be in his place, and that he
envied him to be able to study at the feet of Solomon ben Isaac. He
told us . . ."

She stopped. What had come over her? She had kept up this
steady stream of words just to say something, feeling it wouldn't do to
say nothing. Her intention had not been to indulge in idle chatter. A
chatterbox, a magpie, that's what Obadiah would think of her. Surely he
was about to reply that Gauthier's feelings were of no interest to him.
But Obadiah didn't say anything at all. He just stood there, facing her,
looking a little angry or worried, she wasn't sure which. She thought
maybe he had turned slightly red.

She became aware that the class was perfectly silent, and that
the boys were staring at her. They stared at her while she stared at her
feet, which stuck out from beneath her dress. She thought to herself
that those feet she was staring at would do well to start walking and get
her out of this place. Now. Right now. She tightened her cloak around
her body.

The birds were singing in the courtyard, and even the frogs were
croaking away in their pond. The boys seemed amazed at the extraordinary scene they were witnessing: their schoolmaster talking, or more

exactly not talking, right there in front of the class, face to face with this girl who on other days just sat quietly in a corner of the vestibule making herself almost invisible.

Without bothering to choose, Elvina took three or four parchments covered with Obadiah's elegant, careful handwriting and handed the others back to him. She thanked him without looking at him, pulled her hood over her head, and ran out.

Chapter
21

Gauthier was on his way out of the town of Troyes. He walked his horse slowly, taking care to avoid the large puddles left by last night's rain, so as to not splash the housewives who flattened themselves up against the houses to make room for him. The housewives didn't seem at all unhappy to be given a chance to admire such a handsome young knight. This was not a sight they got to see every day in the narrow streets of their neighborhood! When Gauthier reached the end of the street, he waved his hand in a final good-bye, then disappeared around the corner.

"He's gone. Let's go back in the house." Elvina said. Then she repeated, a little impatiently, "Come on, we have work to do."

But Fleurdelys had become deaf. Rooted to her spot at the entrance of the courtyard, motionless, a smile of wonder on her face, and her arm still raised for a last good-bye in response to Gauthier's, the little girl whispered dreamily, "Did you see his horse, how tall he is, and what a beautiful color, and such slender legs! Nothing like my father's horses!"

She pursued her dream for a few moments, then said, "He's so polite."

"The horse is polite?" Elvina laughed.

"Not the horse! You're pretending not to understand, but you know perfectly well what I mean. Think of the way he thanked you when you gave him the parchments. And he thanked me, too. I didn't give him any parchments, but still, he thanked me ever so courteously. And when he bowed to me, to say good-bye, I saw the sky reflected in his eyes! How can anyone have such light eyes?"

Elvina burst out laughing. "Such a long speech! Is this my cousin Fleurdelys? I don't recognize her!

Fleurdelys glanced at Elvina from the corner of her eye. "You're making fun of me because you're trying to hide the fact that you feel

exactly the same way. I saw you look at him. When you speak to Gauthier, you become all enthusiastic and lively! You straighten up, your eyes
sparkle! You don't look like that at all when you're arguing with my
brother Samuel. I may be little, but I'm not stupid. And you may not be
aware of it, but you are now redder than a beet!"

Elvina pulled her cousin's long dark braids and pinched her
cheeks.

"Ouch! You're hurting me! Stop!" Fleurdelys cried.

Elvina laughed. She lifted Fleurdelys, who was as light as a
feather, up in the air and whirled her around a few times before setting
her back on her feet. Then she kissed her cheek and pulled her hair
again, just for good measure. Finally, a little out of breath, she said, "No,
you are far from stupid. Gauthier is a handsome and noble knight, thoroughly kind and courteous, no one can deny that."

Then, seriously, she added, "And I'm sure that he will always be
a sincere friend of the Jews."

Chapter

22

If only this week could last forever, Elvina thought. If only this morning could last forever, with our house filled with happy, loving voices, and laughter, and the joy we feel at being all together, safe, and healthy. Her mother and grandmother were talking softly as they prepared potions in case other children became ill. Zipporah was grumbling that she had too much work. Aunt Yochebed was warning little Isaac not to place his feet on top of one another while he washed them because this would make him lose his memory. Baby Hannah was babbling as she snuggled on Elvina's lap. The baby was all soft and warm, and as curly as a lamb. Fleurdelys was singing a song to a cat as she pet him, and Samuel and Yom Tov, having wolfed down as many *matzot* as they could eat, were now reciting to each other, as fast as possible, the Mishnah they were supposed to memorize today. Finally, above all the other voices was the strong, cheerful voice of Uncle Meir, who was eating a large piece of cheese with a hearty appetite and washing it down with hot wine. As he ate he told of his dream that he was being attacked by a large bull.

"And do you know what this dream means?" he asked.

No one did, of course, not even Samuel, who always knew everything. Yom Tov was gazing admiringly at his uncle and waiting to hear the answer. Uncle Meir put down his cheese and rubbed his hands together.

"This dream was sent to me by the Prince of Dreams to let me know that my sons will vie with each other in the study of Torah. So, Isaac, study hard! Your brother Samuel is already very learned. Almost a master!"

This didn't bother little Isaac one bit. He was busy wiping his feet with a towel while chewing on a piece of matzah with dried figs. "Samuel is more learned than I am, but he is much older. I'll catch up!" he answered with his mouth full.

"These are words I like to hear!"

Solomon ben Isaac had entered the room with the quick step of a young man. His cloak was pushed back on his shoulders, his eyes were shining, his hair and beard seemed silvery rather than gray.

"As I was crossing the courtyard," he added, "I heard people having a very good time here! Is there room at this table for an old grandfather?"

Little Hannah flashed a sunny smile at him and tried to grab his beard while prattling away in her own baby language that nobody could understand.

Solomon ben Isaac patted Hannah's hair and also Elvina's. He dipped his finger in the honey and rubbed Hannah's lips with it. His eyes were sparkling and mischievous. "My granddaughter will speak well and her words will be as sweet as honey."

Hannah laughed with delight and licked her lips. The boys moved over to make room for their grandfather, while Yochebed ordered Zipporah to bring a nice cup of warm spicy wine for the master, and fry him some eggs, and be quick about it.

From the far end of the room where she was busy crushing herbs in a mortar, Miriam added, "And don't forget to mix the eggs with honey!"

Zipporah muttered that she didn't need to be told because she had known Master Solomon liked his eggs fried in honey long before Miriam and Yochebed were even born.

Solomon sat down next to Isaac. Everyone at the table remained silent, knowing he was about to speak. "Tell me what you learned yesterday in school," Solomon asked Isaac. "Considering how many boiled eggs your mother is feeding you, you must have an excellent memory!"

"I learned . . ."

Everyone burst out laughing as Isaac hastily swallowed his last mouthful, wiped his face, smoothed his tunic, and stood up, looking important. But Solomon ben Isaac raised his hand, and the laughter stopped. "Go on, son, recite the lesson. We are listening."

Isaac recited, "You watered with your foot."

He sat down. Samuel and Yom Tov started laughing again. "All these elaborate preparations to recite five words!" they cried.

Isaac had blushed very red and seemed on the verge of tears. Solomon ben Isaac silenced the two older boys with a nod. "My grandson has recited very well," he said. "He did not stutter or stumble on the words. Now, Isaac, can you explain what this means?"

"We learned that it means they had to carry buckets in order to water their gardens."

For a brief moment, Elvina thought she could see and hear Godolias, the skinny little fox who had dashed out of the wall and into the classroom the previous day. But her grandfather was speaking again.

"You have remembered the lesson very well. In Egypt, you had to rouse yourself from your sleep and toil, carrying heavy pails of water. But in the Promised Land, which drinks the water of the rain of heaven, you will be able to sleep soundly on your beds. What do you think about that?" Solomon pinched Isaac's cheek.

Isaac was so proud he was speechless. Elvina knew exactly how he felt. All of Solomon ben Isaac's grandchildren had felt that same pride when they were little. How many children could boast of receiving personal explanations from the great Solomon of Troyes!

There was silence all around the table; the whole family was looking at the little boy, sharing his pride and his pleasure. Then, his eyebrows puckered from the effort he was making to remember correctly, he asked, "Can I repeat this explanation in school? Can I explain that in Egypt we had to get up early, but in the Promised Land we will all be able to sleep as late as we wish because it will be raining?"

This time the whole family roared with laughter, Solomon ben Isaac not the least of them all. "Don't looked miffed, my boy, we are laughing because we love you and, yes, you can repeat this explanation in school," he said, still laughing.

"In school, where you would do well to run off to this very moment," Yochebed added. "I'm sure Master Obadiah has already started the lesson. Samuel, Yom Tov, off you go, and take Isaac with you."

Chapter 23

The Pesach week went much too fast, my dear Mazal. My uncle, my aunt, and my cousins left this morning for Ramerupt. Just before they left, when their wagon and horses were already waiting in the courtyard, Marguerite's and Jeanne's father, Master Hubert, appeared, looking very jolly. He was carrying several cakes carefully wrapped in linen cloth, which he handed to my grandfather. "Master Solomon," he said, "this year I informed myself! Not like last year when I came a day too early, your Passover wasn't finished, and you couldn't accept my treats!"

He didn't leave time for my grandfather to thank him. I saw my mother and my aunt exchanging knowing glances, as if to say that when Master Hubert starts talking there's no stopping him. "My daughters," he went on, "baked these cakes especially for Master Solomon and his family. They used the best wheat flour, honey, and eggs! You'll love them! I am not about to forget the time Master Solomon cured four of my cows from the disease that had already carried off two of them. Without him I would have lost all of my cows. I owe Master Solomon and, as I said, I am not about to forget it!"

Then he turned to me. "We don't see Master Solomon's granddaughter as often as we used to. My daughters miss you. Why don't you come and play with our little lambs and pick our cherries in the spring?"

"Of course, I'll come," I answered. "Jeanne and Marguerite have always been good friends to me, and just last week . . ."

A sharp glance from my grandfather stopped me. I had told him about the incident of the horseman. Anyway, Master Hubert had already started talking again. "I know what you're thinking. You think things have changed since the passage of Peter the Hermit. Allow me to tell you that you are wrong. My family and I have only good feelings toward you. I'll give you an example. One morning last week we woke up to find one of our geese had been slaughtered. Decapitated in our very courtyard. Our servant was grumbling that for sure it was the Jews who had played that mean trick on us. Well, you should have seen how I shut her up! She's not about to forget it, believe me!"

No one knew what to say, except my grandfather, of course. He answered calmly and courteously, as is his habit. "Master Hubert, we know very well that our Christian neighbors, with whom we have always been on friendly terms, never wished us any harm. As for my granddaughter, as you can see, she is growing up. She is busier and busier around the house. Her mother needs her."

Solomon ben Isaac always says exactly the right thing. I smiled at Master Hubert and Master Hubert smiled back at me. "I had not come to speak of disagreeable topics," he said. "Just to bring the cakes as tokens of our gratitude and friendship."

My grandmother walked up to him to thank him. "Your gift couldn't have come at a better time. We're going to eat the cakes together, the whole family, before our travelers start off on their journey."

Master Hubert smiled broadly, showing every tooth that was left in his mouth. "Very good, very good. Don't forget the biggest slice goes to Master Solomon."

We all laughed, and, I must admit, were thrilled to see him leave. But how sad it was, just a short while later, when the time came to kiss my aunt Yochebed good-bye and help her climb up on the wagon with little Hannah! Solomon ben Isaac blessed the travelers one by one, taking each one's head in both his hands. My mother and grandmother bustled about, making sure that the bottom of the wagon was covered with a nice thick layer of fresh straw to absorb the shocks on bumpy roads. Zipporah piled up provisions of food on every available space she could find on the wagon. The horses whinnied, the neighbors ran in to pay their respects to my uncle Meir and my aunt Yochebed, then just stood there waiting to watch them leave.

Fleurdelys had slipped her hand in mine. I had become used to feeling that soft little hand slipping into mine several times a day. I had become used to sweet-tempered Fleurdelys following me around and keeping me company. I was going to miss her! I felt sorry that I had made fun of her every morning, when she unraveled her protective scarf from her head while throwing worried glances at my own tangled hair, as if she were afraid of seeing . . . I don't know what. I felt sorry for making fun of her the day she proudly informed me she hadn't broken any of the three eggs she had "hatched" this past winter, keeping them warm just as her mother had shown her, wrapped up against her body, but not so tightly as to crush them. "And guess what!" she had said. "Three lovely chicks came out of them!" She was so proud. And I hadn't resisted the mean satisfaction of declaring that I hated little chicks and always broke or crushed the eggs my mother had tried to make me hatch. I saw my sweet little cousin's eyes fill with tears, so I hugged her and told her not to listen to me, that I was a strange girl, not like other girls. She looked me straight in the eye and said, "You are strange, but you're my cousin and I love you."

Hand in hand she and I now watched Samuel lift up his little brother Isaac, kiss him good-bye, and sit him down in the wagon next to his mother. Then my aunt Yochebed called, "Fleurdelys! You're the last one! Kiss your cousin and let's go!"

In just a few moments Fleurdelys would not be with me anymore. I dashed back into the house, shot upstairs like an arrow, opened my chest, took out my fur vest, and ran back down.

Fleurdelys was about to climb up into the wagon. I made her stop and slip on the vest, which was much too large for her. She seemed so surprised that I had to explain. "This belonged to our aunt Rachel. If you knew her as I do, you would love her as I do. This vest is too small for me, so I'm giving it to you. Take good care of it."

My mother smiled at me, one of those adoring tearful smiles that mothers specialize in. Then I started to cry. My mother and my aunt also began to cry, causing my grandmother to launch into a long list of all the dangers awaiting travelers on the roads and in the forests: wolves, boars, bears, and bandits lurking behind every tree.

Fleurdelys, who was finally climbing up into the wagon, turned around and said under her breath, so that I was the only one to hear, "Watch her wring her hands!"

I pinched Fleurdelys's leg as a sign of our mutual understanding.

From the corner of my eye, I saw my father bidding my uncle farewell, then hurrying off. He was busy making a clean copy of my grandfather's commentaries for our brothers in Worms, in Germany, who have requested it. During the week of Pesach, my father had to interrupt his writing, and I knew he wanted to start working again.

"Elvina! I almost forgot! Grab this! Quick!" My aunt Yochebed's eyes were laughing. Bending down from the wagon she handed me an object she had just taken out of her sleeve. A mirror! A beautiful round polished silver mirror! The frame was entirely chiseled with a motif of leaves and fruit, all intertwined. I could see my eyes, my rather long eyelids, which go up a little at the sides, my nose, which is quite delicate, and my mouth, which had a huge smile on it. I had never seen such a smooth, clear mirror, or such a pretty one. "Is this for my mother?" I asked.

Aunt Yochebed laughed. "No, stupid! It's for you! It's a present. But this mustn't prevent you from polishing the Sabbath plate."

I grabbed my aunt's hands, which was all I could reach of her, and kissed them at least twenty times. My very own mirror!

My aunt was laughing. "It belonged to my grandmother, Solomon ben Isaac's mother, of blessed memory, a charitable and pious lady, completely devoted to her family, although I must say she was just a little tiny bit vain. I think that's where you get it from."

Again she wiped a few tears, as did my mother. We escorted the wagon all the way out of town and into the fields, then we watched it disappear into the forest. After that, we turned back. My grandfather placed his arm around Samuel's shoulders to comfort him. Yom Tov walked next to them, looking solemn. He was probably thinking that he was lucky not to have to leave his parents in order to study.

In spite of our sadness, we admired the apple trees and the cherry trees, which were in full bloom and filled the air with their sweet smells. We all stopped under an apple tree and spent a long moment looking up at the sky through the branches. I felt a little dizzy. I thought how nice it would be to drown in all those petals, to be pulled up and engulfed in the amazing softness of the sky and the blossoms.

"Elvina, come out of your dream!" My mother was watching me. She seemed amused to see me so lost in contemplation.

Then my grandfather said, "I understand my granddaughter. There are few things in the world that are as beautiful and as touching as a blossoming tree. Few sights gladden the human soul as does a fruit tree in full bloom. We must give thanks to the Almighty." He then recited, "Blessed be He who has not left anything out in His world and has provided beautiful creatures and beautiful trees for the pleasure of humankind."

We all answered, "Amen."`

"It is a blessing that our sages of blessed memory recommend we recite during the month of Nisan, when we see trees in bloom," my grandfather added.

None of us was in any hurry to go home. I took my new mirror out of my sleeve and had fun looking at the beautiful colors reflected in it. The blue of the sky was speckled with the tiny white flowers. I asked my mother whether it would be possible to embroider white petals on blue cloth, and if it would be as pretty. To make a belt, for example.

"You can try," was her answer. "But embroidery has never been your strong point and I'm inclined to think that you will give up long before you finish your belt."

She's right.

Chapter
24

The weather was so beautiful that Elvina went out without putting on her cloak or slipping into her heavy clogs. Instead, she tied on some leather shoes, with long straps. She walked fast, shaking her head now and then. A light cool wind lifted up the strands of hair escaping from her braids. When I am a married woman, she thought, I will have to cover my head. I will no longer be able to feel the wind in my hair. So enjoy it, girl, she said to herself, enjoy the wind in your hair while you can!

She lifted her skirt a little and walked fast, for the pleasure of feeling free and light on her feet, in spite of some not very good news on this lovely morning. Toby, who had become David, seemed to be out of danger, even though his skin was still very red. But three other children had fallen ill: cute little Belleassez, Tova's daughter, who had just taken her first steps; a two-year-old boy from the neighborhood; and Jacquet, sturdy, chubby Jacquet! Miriam and Precious ran from house to house, from child to child, their baskets full of potions on their arms.

The neighborhood was bustling with activity. Pesach was over. The doors and shutters were wide open. Soups simmered in huge pots, hanging on tripods, in front of house doors. Women were hard at work in their vegetable gardens, straightening up their backs once in a while and exchanging news from one small garden to another. The rich smell of earth being dug up mixed with the aroma of slowly cooking leeks and turnips. Old women were warming up their bones in the sun, sitting on their stools and spinning, their distaffs solidly wedged under their left arms. And how the tongues wagged!

Before even reaching the corner of Market Street, Elvina heard the loud murmur coming up from the market. The sweet warm smell of buns reached her nostrils. This smell was never so enticing as after the long week of Passover without bread or cake. And never had the shelves of the cake and biscuit merchant seemed so appetizing.

"Elvina! At last! I hope you were on your way to our house."

"We haven't seen you in a hundred years!"

"When your cousin Fleurdelys is in town you don't give us a thought. What kind of a friend are you?"

"How can you forget your own students? Shame on you."

Elvina was grabbed, hugged, and smothered by the twins. In turn, she pinched them and kissed their round soft cheeks. All three of them laughed and danced a little, their arms entwined around one another's waists. As always when she saw Rachel and Naomi, Elvina felt happy and lighthearted, as if, at that moment, nothing else existed in the world except their eyes, which sparkled with fun and mischief!

"I never forget you, you silly girls! I was busy, that's all. I still am. Your cousin Toby, whose name is now David, is almost cured, thank God, but other children are ill. I'm in charge of preparing a saffron ointment to spread on their necks and chests."

"Please, Elvina, can we help you?" Rachel jumped up and down with excitement. "It would be such an opportunity for us to learn! What should we do? Tell us!"

"To begin with, if you happen to own red scarves, or pieces of red cloth, bring them to me. Red cloth is rare and precious, and my mother has the hardest time finding some. She wraps her little patients in it to prevent the fever from burning them too much, as it is a red fever that is devouring them."

"Our cousin Muriel received a red scarf as a gift," said Rachel. "We'll bring it to you. If she were here, she would lend it to you, I'm sure. But we want to learn to prepare the ointments."

Naomi started shaking her sister. "Have you already forgotten? We had a question to ask Elvina!" She turned toward Elvina. "The truth is, we were looking for you."

Rachel had stopped laughing. "We had a dream. We wish to know what it means."

"My uncle Meir is the one who can explain dreams. But did I hear you correctly? The two of you had a dream? Does that mean you had the same dream?"

"Yes. Last night. The angel who sends dreams to humans sent us the same dream."

"Have you told anyone about that dream?"

"Of course not! We didn't want to risk having someone give us a wrong interpretation or turning it into a bad omen. We only talked about it together when we woke up."

"Tell me the dream."

Naomi said, very seriously, "Last night we both dreamed we carried a live bird in our arms."

"Did the bird fly away?" Elvina asked.

This time Rachel spoke. "No. It didn't fly away. It was just the opposite. We were keeping the bird warm by holding it close to our hearts."

Elvina burst out laughing. "That's an easy one. I heard my uncle explain it several times. It means you will soon be married."

"You're making fun of us, which is really not nice."

"I'm not making fun. Dreams are no joking matter."

The two pretty little faces were now drained of all their usual cheerfulness. Naomi had turned as white as a turnip. Rachel's eyes were full of tears. Elvina hugged them both and kissed them. "Don't cry. It won't happen tomorrow. But a girl's fate is to get married. All girls get married."

"Not us!" The twins screamed in unison.

"Or else we'll marry the same man," Naomi added.

"We don't want to ever be separated, you understand?" Rachel explained.

Elvina looked at them and saw that they were really worried.

"Two brothers will be found for you," she reassured them, "two brothers living right next to each other, just like your aunt's husband, Joseph ben Simon, and his brother, Nathan ben Simon."

The twins' faces had already brightened up. "That's it! What a good idea!"

"But not right away!"

"No, no, not right away!" The three girls burst out laughing.

They didn't laugh long. A thick voice rose from the ground, almost from under their feet. "You can laugh little misses," the voice said. "You haven't seen what I've seen."

The old beggar drooled and grinned, as usual, but in his eyes

Elvina recognized the terror she had seen in those same eyes last year when the Crusaders marched through the town. The old man lifted himself up on his elbow. "I saw a lamb whose throat had been slit."

"A lamb? Where? Who did it?" The twins spoke together. Their eyes were full of horror.

Elvina was speechless. Her heart was pounding. She thought: the cat, the goose, now a lamb.

"It was over by the forge, in the field. Who did it? How would I know? Forge Street is always deserted. I crawled over here as fast as I could. Here, at least, there are people," the old beggar said.

Elvina shivered. "Come to our house, if you want. Zipporah will give you some soup and hot wine. You'll feel better."

Rachel and Naomi slipped their arms under Elvina's and pulled her away. "Forget this old man and his horrible stories. Let's go make some ointment for the poor little children who are being devoured by the red fever. And on our way, we'll stop and say hello to the spice merchant's donkey. But look! Someone beat us to it!"

A fragile looking blond girl had put her arms around the donkey's head and was pressing her face against his nose. She seemed to be talking to him, and the donkey was bending down, or rather folding down his long ears as if the better to listen to her.

Elvina recognized her right away. "Columba!"

The girl whirled around as if caught doing something wrong. She jumped away from the donkey. Elvina walked up to her. "Columba, don't run off! We're your friends. Tell me, how was your Pesach?"

"Very nice, thank you," the girl answered in a barely audible voice.

Elvina smiled. "I'm happy to see you. You may not believe this, but a whole day and night went by before I discovered your small parchment in my sleeve. Imagine my surprise! I admire your handwriting. It's beautiful! I can see you're just like me, you like to write. Where did you learn?"

Columba didn't answer. The suspicious manner in which she was staring at the twins didn't escape Elvina.

"Naomi and Rachel are my students," she explained. "They're my friends, and they will be your friends, too. So now, tell us. In Germany, do all the girls learn to write as well as you do?"

Columba had regained some composure. "Not all of them."

Her voice was clear and musical and pleasant to listen to. It reminded Elvina of Gauthier's flute playing. "In our family," Columba explained, "girls learn to read and to write very early. Just like the boys."

But then her voice broke off, as if it was having a hard time coming out of her throat. "I meant to say that they used to learn to read and write, that my cousins and I used to learn . . ." She was speaking with increasing difficulty, but she forced herself. She sounded like someone reciting a lesson. "My cousins and I learned together, Matriona was the oldest and I was the youngest. Bona was in the middle. She looked very much like you, Elvina. She was tall and dark haired, like you. And she had a kind heart, like you."

Suddenly Columba choked, buried her face in her hands, and sobbed. Her whole body shook. Never had Elvina and her friends been witnesses to such violent grief.

They put their arms around her, they patted her head, they stroked her back. Rachel and Naomi had started to cry, too. Women walked by, their baskets on their arms, and stared at the group of weeping girls.

Little by little Columba calmed down. She wiped her eyes with her scarf. Rachel took a bun out of her sleeve and handed it to Columba. "Here, eat this. It got a little crushed, but it's still delicious. I baked it myself this morning with nice rye flour, honey, and dates left over from Pesach."

Columba sniffled, smiled, and nibbled the edge of the squashed bun. Elvina took her arm and pulled her very gently. "Let's go a little further away, where people won't notice us so much. What happened to your cousins Bona and Matriona?"

"They died," Columba whispered, so low that the three girls had to stand very close to her. "Their parents died, too. And their little brother. Their father was my mother's brother. The Crusaders killed them. They also killed our grandfather, who was a great scholar. After that, my parents decided to accept . . ."

She looked up at Elvina, as if imploring her. Elvina gave her a quick hug. "I understand. Don't say another word; it causes you too much pain. Were you shopping when we met you?"

"Yes, but . . ."

"But what?"

"But the women push me around, and the merchants make fun of me and insult me. My mother doesn't dare come out. She thinks they won't be as cruel to me because I am a girl and small for my age. She forbids me to go to non-Jewish merchants because we want to live here as good Jews. But I'm always scared. Some merchants refuse to sell me anything and some throw fruit or meat at me, as if I were a dog." Columba shook her head sadly. "You can't possibly understand. This town is your home."

It didn't take Elvina long to decide what she was going to do. "I'll accompany you to the shops and tell the merchants you're my friend. Nobody refuses Solomon ben Isaac's granddaughter."

Naomi and Rachel were enthusiastic. "Good idea! We'll go with you. Columba, what do you need to buy?"

"Barley for porridge, and vegetables for soup. Honey. Cardamom and aniseed to make a potion. And eggs. We own two hens, but we need more eggs than they can give us."

"Let's start with honey and spices," decided Elvina.

"Ginger for the digestion! Cinnamon for the eyes!"

They could hear the spice merchant's strong, cheerful voice before they even reached his shop. As soon as he caught sight of Elvina, he called out, "But a beautiful young plant like you doesn't need any of that! To what do I owe the pleasure of your visit? Tell me."

"I need some saffron."

"It so happens I have some that has just been brought to me from Spain, such a rich color, you've never seen the like, powdered gold . . ."

He stopped in the middle of his sentence as he noticed Columba. Elvina took her by the hand and led her right into the shop. Rachel and Naomi followed. Several women made way for them and stared in amazement. Elvina looked the merchant straight in the eye. "This young stranger is my friend. You will be doing me a great favor if you treat her well."

The spice merchant bowed, but he was frowning. "The granddaughter of our master Solomon ben Isaac knows what she is doing, I'm sure, and our master Solomon knows what he is doing when he is protecting this family."

A woman in the shop declared in a loud voice, "Our master Solomon knows what he is doing, but several children have been stricken with the fever."

Another housewife emphatically nodded her agreement. "There are ugly things going on, and even though my husband has ordered me to mind my own cooking and spinning, I have eyes and I have ears."

A third woman, a farmwife who had come in to barter eggs for saffron, exclaimed, "Well, what do you know! I recognize this girl! Just the other day she asked me if I could sell her an egg freshly laid by a black hen, and not only that, but it had to be the black hen's first egg. I told her I didn't do business with witches."

Columba seemed ready to faint, and the twins were looking at their new friend with a mixture of fear and wonder. Elvina felt shaken.

"My friend would like some honey, and I need saffron," she said very quickly.

Chapter
25

*M*azal, dear Mazal, how can people be so cruel to a little girl who has done them no harm?

Columba explained to us that it is a German custom to give a small boy the first egg laid by a black hen in order to improve his memory. Since Godolias has now started learning with Obadiah, their mother told Columba to find such an egg. It seemed strange to us, but Columba assured us that it is very common in Germany.

I forced the merchants to stop being mean to Columba, even if they don't go so far as to treat her nicely. We went to see the woman who sells fruits and vegetables. She doesn't have much to offer in this season, but Columba's family hasn't had the time yet to plant a garden, and Columba has no choice but to buy the turnips, leeks, and cabbage the family needs.

The only one to be nice, actually, was the apothecary. Just as we were entering his shop Columba became terrified and hid behind me. You have to admit, he's scary looking, with his huge red beard and his fat fingers! I held Columba's hand to reassure her while she was explaining what she wanted: cardamom, aniseed, vinegar, and also some mint and parsley.

"Is someone vomiting or having seizures?" he asked. "Do you have a person in your house who is restless and troubled?" He was genuinely interested.

Columba seemed embarrassed and confused. She hadn't expected all those questions. She answered, "No, I mean yes, what I mean is my father has lost his appetite."

"For that, you only need cardamom and aniseed. And you're in luck, because I crushed and mixed some with vinegar just a couple of days ago."

"My mother has ordered me to buy mint and parsley, also."

The twins and I walked Columba part of the way, but she did not allow us to go all the way to her door. From her house, there rose the sound of hammering, which seemed to answer the sounds coming from Dieulesault's forge next door. Columba explained that her father and older brother were busy fixing the house. "Back in Germany, my father used to be a scribe. He copied several Torah scrolls. He's the one who taught me to read and write."

She was standing very straight and proud, and her eyes were shining. But it didn't last. She was quiet for a moment, and then she said, sadly, "The Torah scrolls were burned by the Crusaders in our synagogue. In Mainz, my brother studied day and night with the great teachers of our community. So he's not very good with his hands. Neither is my father. At first, Dieulesault helped them. He still lends them tools, but we can see that he does it reluctantly, and that makes us sad."

I then walked Rachel and Naomi home and they gave me their cousin Muriel's red scarf. Muriel is staying with their sister, Bella, whose baby is due any moment.

I promised the twins that some day soon I would teach them to mix potions, then I ran home. My mother had just arrived. As I walked in the door, she cried, "Elvina! Wash your hands! I beg you! Before you have anything to eat, wash your hands!"

"You're getting to be more and more like your sister Yochebed," I laughed. "Didn't you hear Uncle Meir, explaining that the wicked Shibbeta, the strangler of children, does not haunt our regions?"

"Hush, girl! If you had spent your entire morning sitting with sick children, if you had felt their burning foreheads and seen their red swollen eyes, if you had heard them croaking feebly, like poor weak little crows, and then start to cough and choke, you would not be laughing!"

She was really worried and tired, so I rushed up to her and kissed her.

"Did you bring the saffron?" she asked.

"I have the saffron. And I'll prepare the ointment with rose oil and ashes. I'll pound the ashes until I get a fine powder, then I'll mix it with the rose oil and beat it until it turns into a nice soft paste. So you see, you can rely on me. But now, you and I are going to eat. Zipporah will serve us some soup and some spicy hot wine. Then you will rest and I will take care of everything. And first, of course, we will wash our hands."

My mother smiled an exhausted but happy smile. "One would think you were the mother and I the daughter!"

That's certainly what I thought but I didn't let on. I took some hot water from the stove and brought a pitcher and basin to my mother. Zippo-rah set down a large bowl of steaming hot soup with pieces of meat in it on the table. We were just beginning to dip our bread into the soup when, look-ing out of the open window, I saw my grandfather crossing the courtyard. He was practically running and seemed beside himself. My mother called to him and he came into our house.

"A thief has broken into the synagogue! He cut the margins from a magnificent book that doesn't even belong to us! It must have happened during the night, and maybe even before Pesach. No one looked at the book during the Passover week."

I was bringing him a bowl of soup and I almost dropped it. The margins of a book! And here I had forgotten all about the strip of parch-ment found by the twins! That's what it was! A carefully cut margin! So was Columba's little note!

It was all I could do to put the bowl down on the table and repeat like an idiot, "Cut the margins of a book?"

Solomon ben Isaac was so upset he was shaking. He didn't notice that my own voice was very unsteady. He started to gulp down his soup without looking at it. "Yes. Very skillfully, too. Whoever did it must be used to handling parchment. The book is now horribly mutilated. It's a copy of the Chapters of Rabbi Eliezer, and it belongs to a rich and pious Jew from Châlons who was kind enough to lend me the volume. Usually he rents it to those who need it, for a high price. I had intended to have a much simpler and less costly copy made for my own use. But now we'll have to spend a huge sum to replace the damaged volume! It will take months, and mean-while how does it make us look? That such a thing could happen in Troyes? In our synagogue?"

I dropped onto the bench next to my grandfather. He ate and talked at the same time, speaking to nobody in particular. "There is someone in our town who needs parchment and didn't come up with any other way of getting it. This someone is as nimble as a cat! The synagogue door is always closed at night. He must have climbed in through the window."

I went upstairs to get the parchment found by Naomi and Rachel. I handed it to my grandfather, explaining where it came from. He spread it out on the table. "Yes! This is one of the stolen margins! And the verses from the prophet Isaiah predict imminent disasters and catastrophes!"

Solomon ben Isaac finished his bowl of soup, rose to his feet, and hurried away to the synagogue, taking the parchment with him.

Now, dear Mazal, I am crushing my powder into my rose oil in the small mortar I use for mixing medicines. The ointment is a beautiful bright red and has a wonderful fragrance thanks to the rose oil. My mother will rub it on the chests of the little patients. They will smell nice, their fever will come down, and their cough will be soothed away. At least I hope so.

I did not mention Columba's note. It too was written on a carefully cut, perfectly smooth strip of parchment. But the skin was less white and less fine. Where did it come from? Another book? Another theft? The margin of a precious volume of the Talmud, or a commentary of one of our great Rabbis?

Was I wrong not to mention it? Should I have betrayed Columba? I can't imagine her stealing anything! I can't imagine her climbing up the wall of the synagogue to the window, which is not only very narrow, but very high up!

Mazal, my Mazal, what is going on? Animals' throats are being slit or their heads chopped off, margins have been stolen, children are being devoured by the fever! Mazal, my Mazal, I'm beginning to be afraid. But afraid of what? Of whom? Of sweet, sad little Columba?

Chapter

26

As they approached the house, they could hear the crying and wailing of the little boy's mother. The boy had just died. Elvina had insisted on accompanying Solomon ben Isaac, but now there was a knot in her stomach and she felt like she might burst into tears. Just as they were about to enter the house, she braced herself. She knew that small children were fragile and too often died before even knowing how to walk or talk. But she had never actually seen the death of a child and the parents' despair.

It was very light in the room because the window was wide open to let the child's soul come and go. A child's soul was like a bird. For several days it fluttered about, close to the house, because it was so hard for a child's soul to leave home. After a few days, angels would take it to Gan Eden, to Paradise, where it would play and learn with other little children who had died.

Elvina glanced rapidly at the bed, on which a tiny form was resting, wrapped up in a piece of linen cloth. The child was exactly little Hannah's size, thought Elvina, and she imagined her cousin, whose soft neck smelled of milk. She imagined Hannah not moving, not waving her hands and wiggling her chubby fingers, not laughing any more. Then her tears started to flow. Through them she could still see some amulets hanging on the bed. Those amulets had not been of any use.

All the people who had come to offer comfort made way for Solomon ben Isaac. Solomon walked straight up to the young father and put his arms around him. The young man sobbed, "Master Solomon! He was my firstborn!"

"Take courage, my son."

"He died in his sleep. He was smiling."

"Your son left this world without having sinned. He will be sitting next to the divine throne."

The young mother was sitting on a bench, supported by two

other women. She started screaming, "I don't care about all that! My son is much too little to go away all alone. He barely knows how to walk! He must be frightened!"

Solomon looked at her, his face reflecting the great pity he felt for her. "Your husband told me the child was smiling. That's because an angel had come down to kiss him. Think of that. He's not afraid."

The child's mother murmured, "Yes, Master Solomon," and sobbed even harder. Elvina saw that her grandfather's eyes were full of tears.

When Elvina and Solomon ben Isaac left the house, Elvina looked up with relief. There was the sky, and there were the big white clouds chasing each other toward countries she would never know. Everything was as usual.

But was everything as usual? A dozen men and women stood waiting for Solomon. The look on their faces terrified Elvina. And yet, several of these faces were familiar to her. There was Simha the *shammash*, and also some Jews from neighboring villages and hamlets, men and women she had seen more than once at the synagogue for the Sabbath services.

She held on to her grandfather's arm as he calmly walked toward the group, showing neither haste nor hesitation. One of the men yelled, "Master Solomon ben Isaac, this time it has gone too far! How many of our children must die before we take the necessary measures?"

"The necessary measures?" Solomon's tone was perfectly courteous. He had stopped walking and stood facing the group of angry people.

"Master Solomon knows very well what we are talking about. This family of false Jews must be sent away!"

"There are no false Jews in our community."

The whole group started speaking at once in loud angry voices.

"Master Solomon, it's easy for you to outsmart us with words. But you know the people we are referring to."

"People who have been sullied by the waters of baptism!"

"Apostates who have left the faith of their ancestors!"

"We want them chased away!"

"Before our children all die, one after the other!"

"Before the earth cracks open!"

"Before the sun becomes dark and owls invade our houses!"

Solomon started. He looked sharply at the crowd. "What did you just say? Where did that come from?"

A man who lived not far from Dieulesault the blacksmith stepped forward. "Parchment strips are raining on our neighborhood. I found one near my house. My cousins, who came in from the country to buy some tools, found one just in front of Dieulesault's shop. A woman found one on her doorstep. I can't read them, but Simha here has read them to us, and I may be an ignoramus, Master Solomon, but I can grasp what it's all about."

Solomon ben Isaac turned toward Simha the *shammash*. Simha looked embarrassed. He shifted from one foot to the other and played with the edge of his hood. "It's just as he said, Master Solomon. For the past few days thin strips of parchment have been pouring like rain on our neighborhood. They're covered with writing, always the same kind of words."

"Do you have them on you?" Solomon asked.

"God forbid, Master Solomon! I buried them. They were burning my hands!"

"I see."

Now Solomon stood up very straight. "In spite of all that," he said, "we will not chase away a family whose repentance is sincere. We shall not show less compassion than the emperor of Germany, who has allowed baptized Jews to return to the religion of their ancestors. Nor shall we go against the decree of our teacher, Rabbenu Gershom, Light of the Exile, who has strictly forbidden us to remind any Jews about their sin after they have repented and returned to their religion."

"Does Master Solomon want us to lose all our children?" a woman cried out.

Elvina, who could read her grandfather's face, saw that he was sorry for the people but would not give in.

"Watch over your children, feed them with greater care than ever. And pray. And remember, I'm telling you once again, chasing this family from our town would be a grave sin."

The women accepted his decision. But three men who had just

arrived from their fields, judging from their dirty tunics and cloaks, torn socks and mud-covered clogs, came to stand right in front of Solomon.

"So maybe we'll chase them away ourselves—these converts who settled here for our misfortune. With due respect, Master Solomon."

Elvina's heart was pounding as she clung to her grandfather's arm. They had succeeded in making Solomon angry, a rare occurrence. He coldly eyed the three men from head to toe, then spoke, hammering out his words. "These Jews belong to a distinguished and respectable German community that has suffered greatly. They are under my protection. Let no one dare cause them the slightest pain. The punishment will be severe. I, Solomon ben Isaac, am warning you!"

There was a moment of heavy silence. Then Solomon spoke again. "As for as the rain of prophecies, with God's help, and also with your help, we will find out where it is coming from."

The men backed up, muttering under their breath. Several women were sniffling and wiping their eyes with their headscarves or their sleeves.

"Master Solomon," one of them begged, "if only we had some good strong amulets to protect our little ones against . . . against . . . you know . . ."

Solomon nodded. "Come to my house in a little while. I will inscribe some verses on parchments for all those who want them. And my wife will give you strengthening herb teas for your children to drink."

Chapter 27

Elvina sat on the bench in the courtyard, crushing up a few eggshells together with cinnamon. Later, she would boil the powder and make a hot beverage for her grandfather, whose eyes had been tired lately. She put down her mortar and pestle next to her on the bench, removed her shoes and stockings, stretched out her legs, and wiggled her toes. Then she shut her eyes to concentrate on the pleasure of feeling the warm sun on her skin. Today was the first day of the month of Iyyar, the day of the New Moon, a day of rest for the daughters of Israel. Unfortunately, there is no rest for women who take care of sick children. Miriam and Precious had left a little later than on other mornings, that's all. But things were looking up. No other child had died. Tova's little girl was hardly feverish at all anymore, and Elvina would soon be able to go see her.

"Can't I go today?" she had asked her mother.

But Miriam was not to be persuaded. "You'll go when little Belleassez is totally cured and we can be certain that the evil spirits have departed. Until then, you will not set foot in that house."

So Elvina was all by herself, very busy enjoying the warmth of the spring sun on her toes.

"Elvina! Are you asleep?"

Yes, she must have dozed off because she didn't see Naomi and Rachel enter the courtyard, and now they were sitting with her on the bench, talking into her ears, one on each side, as was their custom. "What are you doing? Nothing? You don't even have your spinning, or a little embroidery work of the kind you like so much! What are you doing on your bench, doing nothing?"

"Ouch! You're making me deaf! You know very well I hate embroidery, besides, you can see I am doing something. I'm preparing a powder. I plan to use it to brew a tea for my grandfather, for his eyes. Have you forgotten today is a day of rest for women?"

The twins looked sheepish. "We haven't forgotten. Not really forgotten. But if you could explain to us what it's about, it would help. Then we'll tell you something that will interest you."

"I'll tell you what my grandfather has often told me. After the children of Israel came out of Egypt and began wandering in the desert, they asked Aaron to make for them a golden calf that they could worship. In order to make a golden calf, all of the jewels had to be melted. But the women refused to hand over their earrings, their necklaces, and their bracelets. As a reward, the Almighty decreed that the day of the New Moon would be a special day of rest for all of the daughters of Israel. There. That's the story. Now, what do you have to tell me? And please, for once, don't speak at the same time."

So it was Naomi who, standing straight and looking solemn, announced, "There is a thief in our neighborhood! A thief who stole into our house and took a mirror!"

"A mirror?"

"Yes. Our mother and our aunt each own a mirror. They are identical mirrors. They received them from their mother as wedding gifts. Aunt Flora's mirror has been stolen."

"Isn't it possible that she just lost it?" asked Elvina.

"Certainly not," Naomi answered. "She never carries it with her; it never goes out of the house. But she often leaves it on the table in the big room downstairs, next to the window, because she says that's where the light is best to look at herself when she combs her hair or cleans her teeth."

Rachel was becoming impatient and couldn't keep silent any longer. "Come to our house," she now entreated, grabbing Elvina's arm. "Our mother will give you something nice to eat, then we'll all go together to consult Eleazar, the seer."

"The one who lives out in the fields?"

"Yes. He'll tell us where we can find the mirror. Come on! It's a perfect day, the countryside is beautiful, and we'll have fun."

Elvina wasn't quite sure. This was a day of rest and there was nothing to keep her from going for a walk in the country with her friends. But to go visit a seer? What if her father or grandfather heard about it? Both of them firmly condemned those kinds of practices.

"Listen," she said finally, "I'll walk with you, but I will not go in to see him."

"You'll do as you like, but let's go!"

Once they were out on the street, Naomi and Rachel seemed to have agreed between them to walk on either side of Elvina and talk to her nonstop, very fast, about everything under the sun, the stolen mirror, what they were going to eat, the color of the sky, the clouds . . .

They crossed paths with a woman who turned her face the other way. Another woman darted back into her house just as they walked by. The twins were talking faster and faster, louder and louder into Elvina's ears, a dizzying flood of words. A third woman passed them, hurrying by and pretending not to see them.

"Be quiet!" Elvina suddenly yelled and stopped in her tracks.

The twins became silent and looked at her sadly.

"Did you see these women?" Elvina asked them in a lower tone of voice. "They didn't greet me. They've known me forever and they pretended not to recognize me!"

Naomi and Rachel put their arms around Elvina and held her tightly. "Don't pay attention to them! Please, Elvina, don't pay attention!"

"What's going on?" Elvina asked. She could hear the quavering in her own voice. Naomi and Rachel kept pulling her toward their house.

As they pulled her, Rachel explained, "There are people who are angry at your grandfather for protecting the German family. They're afraid for their children. Do you smell the horrible smell floating out of all the windows? Everybody is burning asafetida next to their children's cribs and beds in order to keep away the demons."

"Look at the doors," Naomi added. "Do you see all the amulets, in addition to the *mezuzot* that the Almighty has ordered us to fasten to our doorposts? People are scared. And angry."

"That's why the women aren't speaking to you. But don't worry, they'll get over it," Rachel concluded.

"Solomon ben Isaac will bring them back to their senses," added Naomi.

Elvina clung to that thought. Yes, her grandfather would bring them back to their senses. She wished she could run to him right now! But she didn't want to leave her friends. And she didn't want to walk alone on the streets. Anyway, they had just arrived at the twins' house.

Flora, the twins' aunt, greeted Elvina. Her eyes were red. "Did the girls tell you about my mirror?" she asked. "Such a pretty mirror! My mother's precious gift to me!"

"It looks exactly like this one! Look!" Rachel had run to fetch the other mirror. It was a round mirror, larger than Elvina's, but not as smooth or as polished, and the frame was not as delicately chiseled. The image of herself Elvina saw in it was a little fuzzy, very pale, and not smiling, whereas usually . . .

"Cheer up, Elvina, it will come out all right! Solomon ben Isaac will know what to do."

Elvina started to cry. Rachel explained to Flora and Rosa what had happened. All of them surrounded Elvina, hugged and kissed her and comforted her. "These women are mean! Forget about them! Let's eat some cakes, then we'll go visit Eleazar!"

A little while later they were all following the path that ran alongside the fields. The three girls walked ahead, with the two identical mothers right behind them. The sun was hot, but a cool breeze carried the fragrance of the young tender shoots and freshly plowed earth. Elvina took in several deep breaths and felt more hopeful. Yes, summer was just around the corner, the children would be cured, the neighbors would all be reconciled with each other. Everything would be the same once more.

28

The seer lived in a ramshackle log cabin without any windows. Several *mezuzot* hung from the doorpost, each of them in a strange carved wood sheath. The seer was enjoying the nice weather, sitting in the sun on a low stool. All you could see of him, at first, was an enormous, dirty gray beard, which swept the ground in front of the stool. Eleazar stood up, took one long look at Elvina, and exclaimed, "Unless I am very much mistaken, you are the granddaughter of our master Solomon ben Isaac. Your visit honors me."

Elvina looked so baffled, Eleazar burst out laughing. "I would be a paltry seer if I weren't capable of recognizing those eyes of yours, which are exactly the same as those of our revered master Solomon. Eyes the color of hazelnuts, eyes full of kindness, now merry, now sad, depending on whether his soul is joyful or afflicted. Eyes every bit as alive as a spring sky."

Elvina felt herself blushing with pleasure. Her grandfather's eyes!

The seer was not finished. "I know your grandfather well. He does me the great honor of paying me a visit now and then."

Elvina had obviously failed in her efforts to conceal her astonishment, causing the old seer to roar with laughter. "You can't believe it, can you?"

Elvina was embarrassed. "No, well, yes, of course, I mean . . ."

Eleazar laughed again. "What you mean is that Solomon would never consult a seer. But follow me, all of you, follow me. And mind the snakes! They are stretching their bodies and warming themselves in the sun after a long cold winter, just as human beings do."

They all followed as he led them to the other side of his cabin. "Now, you understand?" he asked Elvina.

It was Elvina's turn to burst out laughing. A swarm of bees was buzzing around a huge and thriving beehive. Elvina laughed and clapped her hands, then turned to her friends, who were staring at her as if she had suddenly gone mad. "There is nothing my grandfather likes better than honey."

The old seer had stopped laughing. He straightened himself up and spoke respectfully. "It is a fact. Our master Solomon ben Isaac is very fond of honey. And he is not too proud to walk across a few fields to come and visit old Eleazar and eat some of his honey because he knows it is the best in the whole region." He smiled proudly.

He now turned to Flora and Rosa. "And you two, why have you come? I imagine you have a reason."

Flora took out her mirror from her sleeve. "We have come to consult the most capable Eleazar. A mirror was stolen from us. A mirror exactly like this one." She spoke shyly.

Eleazar took the mirror and examined it. Flora explained, "The mirror was on the table in our downstairs room. It must have been stolen shortly after sunrise, before my sister and I came downstairs. The men had already left for the synagogue and the servant had gone to draw water from the well. The children were still asleep."

"We shall consult the wax. Come in," Eleazar invited them.

Elvina had forgotten her resolve to stay outside and wait for her friends. She followed them into the seer's small dark cabin.

A lone, wretched lamp was burning in a corner, its light faltering. Eleazar took a candle, set it down on a stool and, using a long stick, drew a circle on the dirt floor, all around the stool. He then looked at the girls.

"Which one is the youngest of you all? You can only question the Prince of Wax through the intermediary of a pure young creature."

He considered the twins. "How old are you?"

"Eleven."

"Much too old. I need a child of less than nine years. We shall have to ask the neighbors' son. He is tending his sheep not far from here."

Eleazar went to the door and let out a powerful whistle. Then he invited his visitors to sit around the stool, just outside the circle.

"Master Eleazar needs me?" A boy, about seven years old, stood in the doorway. He was a stocky, dirty, disheveled, and very jolly child.

"Master Eleazar will reward me, just like last time?" he grinned.

"Yes, yes. You shall sit on my lap, in front of this candle, and I shall tell you what you must say and do. We are searching for one who has stolen a mirror."

Eleazar closed the door. It became very dark. The seer lit the candle, using the lamp, then sat down and placed the boy on his lap. The flame trembled then rose. For a while, no one spoke. Only the faces were lit up. Elvina could see Rosa and Flora biting their lips. Rachel and Naomi were gaping, their eyes wide open.

Finally, Eleazar asked the boy, "What do you see?"

"Nothing."

"Repeat after me: Adam Havah Abton Absalom Sarfiel Nuriel Daniel."

One by one, the boy repeated the seven names.

"Now," ordered Eleazar, "touch the candle with your finger and say, 'By these seven names, I conjure you to appear in the wax of this candle and to answer me the truth.'"

The boy placed a grimy finger on the candle and began slowly to repeat the seer's words.

"By these seven names . . ."

"By these seven names . . ."

"I conjure you . . ."

"I conjure you . . ."

A trail of liquid wax slowly made its way down the side of the candle, forming long twisted shapes as it cooled.

Elvina couldn't take her eyes off the soft trail of wax, brightly reflecting the flame, as it wriggled and writhed. The trail of wax rippled and grew, and Elvina started to feel soft and sluggish as if she, too, were made of warm wax. She felt she might doze off.

"Now, do you see something?" Eleazar asked the boy.

"I see a wax woman leaning against the candle."

"She is sent by the Prince of Wax. Say to her, 'Come in peace.'"

"Come in peace," the boy repeated obediently.

"Is this woman clothed in a long shiny dress?" Eleazar asked.

"Yes."

"Command her to dance!"

"Dance!" said the little shepherd. Then he laughed.

"Don't laugh! Tell me, is the wax woman dancing?"

"Yes, Master Eleazar, she's dancing."

"Ask her where the mirror has been hidden, the mirror that has been stolen from Flora, who is here in person, requesting an answer."

The boy repeated the question.

Again there was a long silence. Elvina had come out of her stupor. Her stomach had suddenly tied up into a knot. She wished she could leave, go back out into the daylight. She was sorry she had come in, she didn't want to know anything more; she just wanted to run away, far from this old man with a beard that swept the ground. She did not want to be an accomplice to his invocations, which, she was sure, were a sin. She didn't even want to know the results. Sweat trickled down her back. All she could think was: Get out of here! But she stayed. She didn't dare stand up, she didn't dare leave the others. She started biting her fingers.

The boy was saying that the woman was not shining any more, that she had become dark. Everything had turned dark and the woman was disappearing.

"Tell her to go in peace," ordered the seer.

"Go in peace," the boy repeated.

It was over. Eleazar set the boy back on his feet, got up, blew out the candle, and opened the door. A great beam of light burst into the room. The seer then turned to Flora. "The mirror is hidden in a very dark place. The thief is a creature of darkness."

Chapter 29

azal, dear Mazal, I am having a hard time falling asleep. I miss my sweet, kind Fleurdelys and Hannah, who used to curl up beside me in a warm little ball. Zipporah's loud snoring, however familiar, is no comfort to me. Comfort from what? How can you ask, Mazal? Didn't you see those women turning away to avoid greeting me?

One woman slammed her window shutter when I passed her house! A little further down the street, another woman was explaining to her neighbors that it was better to leave the shutters ajar to allow the evil spirits to come and go as they pleased; this way they wouldn't get irritated. And then, just as I walked by, she practically yelled, "Nobody's sick in Solomon ben Isaac's house! Don't you find this very strange?"

She had barely finished her sentence when I heard a high-pitched voice telling her not to talk nonsense and not to forget the respect one owes Master Solomon ben Isaac and his family. "You're a great one for talking," the shrill voice said, "but when your children are ill, who do you beg to come and cure them? Mistress Precious and Mistress Miriam."

It was Simonet's wife! I hadn't seen her because she was walking behind me. For the first time in my life, I was thrilled to meet the ferret-faced woman! Is it possible that you sent her, Mazal?

I know, Mazal, I know what you are saying: all of this will teach me not to be so proud. I must remember that on more than one occasion my grandfather was very happy to have Simonet at his side, Simonet who is as strong as a boar and entirely devoted to my grandfather.

I had not allowed the twins to escort me home. I refused to admit that I was scared. I'm used to walking alone in the streets of our town, and I wished to face, with my head held high, those who would dare slander my grandfather. But, in spite of all that, I was relieved to have the ferret's company for a while!

So, dear Mazal, that's where matters stand right now! And the streets reek of asafetida; it makes you choke! It seems to me that the *mazzikim*, who have no shadows, but have ears and eyes and especially noses, must be getting the message! Such a disgusting smell!

Just as I arrived home, two horsemen were leaving our courtyard. I found my grandmother in tears. My grandfather, as usual, was trying to calm her. "Come, my poor Precious, you'll frighten the children. I will only be away for a week. The roads leading to Châlons are heavily frequented, the weather is fine, the days are getting longer, and the two horsemen escorting me are strong men armed with trusty swords and sharp knives. I'm considering taking Dieulesault along, too. And, you mustn't forget, the Almighty will watch over me."

The horsemen had been sent by the community of Châlons to fetch my grandfather. The Jewish community of Châlons is being torn by violence of a nature not unrelated to the troubles we are experiencing here in Troyes. In Châlons, two families have been fighting right in the synagogue! Each family is accusing the other of descending from people who submitted to baptism!

My grandfather could hardly contain his indignation. "I am told those two families have gone out of control. They come to blows at every opportunity, wherever they may find themselves. When they meet at the market, even the women spit at one another and tear off each other's head-dresses to show their contempt."

"Grandfather, will you tell them about Rabbenu Gershom's decree?" I asked.

"Yes," he replied. "Rabbenu Gershom of Mainz, who was the master of my masters, was extremely strict concerning that question. His decree forbids us, under the penalty of being banned from the Jewish community, to utter insulting words to apostates who have repented—in other words, to Jews who allowed themselves to be baptized and then decided to return to their brothers. It is also forbidden to insult their descendants."

He shook his head sadly. "But if they are sending for me it is because the truly great ones, those who were worthy of resolving this conflict, lost their lives last year in Mainz, in Worms, and in Speyer. The situation here in Troyes is also of great concern to me. Our brothers are worried about their children. I understand them, but I will not give in. Then there is the one who steals margins. Who can it be? And now Obadiah has come to inform me that three more children are stricken with the fever."

As I listened to my grandfather, I studied his face. All these worries had darkened it, as a cloud darkens the sky. And yet, behind the dark cloud, Solomon ben Isaac's eyes were twinkling. "My grandfather appears to me to be sad and joyful at the same time," I remarked. "I believe the prospect of a trip rather pleases him. And he will see my dear aunt Rachel!"

Solomon ben Isaac laughed and pinched my cheek. "How well my granddaughter knows me! Yes, I will be very happy to see Rachel, my little one. And I must admit that the thought of riding through the fields, along the river banks, into the deep woods, which smell of mushrooms and moss, and feeling the cool spring breezes on my old wrinkled forehead does not exactly cause me pain. You'll watch over your grandmother, won't you?"

I promised him I would. But I would so have loved to go to Châlons! I've never been further than Ramerupt.

My grandfather read my thoughts. He stroked my cheek affectionately. "Later, this summer, if the roads are safe, you and your mother might be able to go with a convoy of merchants and visit your aunt Rachel. I'll try to arrange it."

A real trip! On horseback! I jumped for joy and hugged my grandfather, just like a child!

And tomorrow I'll jump out of bed as soon as Simha the *shammash* calls. I want to see Grandfather straddle his horse. He will be setting out at dawn in order to arrive before the Sabbath begins. I intend to give him a short letter I wrote to my aunt Rachel, to tell her that, God willing, we shall see each other soon.

And then I will do my best to comfort my grandmother. She will need it, I'm afraid.

Chapter
30

After Solomon ben Isaac's departure, Precious did not have much time to give over to worrying. Three schoolboys were sick, coughing and burning with fever. One of them was covered with red spots. The mothers did not want anyone but Miriam and Precious by their children's bedsides. The Sabbath was not a very joyful one.

On top of that, Elvina heard from Samuel that Godolias had not been to school in several days. So, Sunday morning, she decided to find out what was the matter.

All was quiet on Forge Street. Dieulesault had left for Châlons with Solomon. Columba's house was closed, as always. Elvina couldn't help wondering what that family did all day long behind their closed door and shuttered window. Once Columba had told Elvina that her mother cried a lot, her father prayed, and they kept the shutter closed and the lamps burning.

But on this Sunday morning, the trapdoor leading to the cellar was not quite shut. Elvina bent over and lifted it a little. As she did, a small familiar voice spoke up from inside her. "Go away, girl, go away, right now!" it said. "Don't you have a lot of spinning to do? Didn't you promise to watch over your grandmother? Weren't you going to study the reading for this coming Sabbath?" Elvina shook her head. "You're trying to scare me," she said to the voice in her head, "but it won't work. I saw Columba come out from this cellar, once. She may be in there right now. Maybe she needs me!"

She lifted the trapdoor. The small voice mustered all the strength it could and yelled, "You're crazy, girl! You're crazy! Since when do you go down into people's cellars? What are you looking for? Go home!" But Elvina wouldn't listen any longer.

Cautiously she started to climb down the ladder. Through the trapdoor, which she had left open, enough daylight came into the cellar for Elvina to see that it was rather large. She saw some clothes, a cloak,

113

a blanket, all thrown into a messy pile on a straw mattress. A lamp had been set on the ground, but it wasn't burning. Elvina's eyes were becoming used to the semi-darkness. She walked toward the lamp. Next to it were two books and several thin strips of what appeared to be expensive parchment. The stolen margins! Next to them were a goose quill and a small box containing ingredients to prepare ink.

Only then did she see the mirror right on top of the pile of clothes. It looked just like Rosa's mirror!

"Bona!"

Elvina spun around. A tall skinny boy had jumped down into the cellar, ignoring the ladder. He moved toward Elvina. She couldn't make out his features very well, since his back was to the daylight. She saw that he was taller than she was, but still without a beard. His hair was very black, long and matted.

"Bona! At long last! I've been waiting for you!" He spoke like Columba, with the same accent.

Elvina took a few steps toward him, but her real goal was to reach the ladder as fast as possible.

"I am not Bona," she said. "My name is Elvina. I'm a friend of Columba's. I didn't know someone was living here. Please forgive me. I'm going to leave now."

The boy stared at her and showed no intention of stepping aside. In his eyes glimmered a strange and unsettling light.

Suddenly Elvina was scared. "I have to go home! Good-bye!" she cried out.

But he was not letting her through. "It's too dangerous. You'll stay here with me; I'll protect you. Besides, as long as we stay here they'll never find us. I'll light the lamp and lock the trapdoor. I have the key."

Elvina was beginning to panic. Why did he want to lock them up? She screamed at the top of her lungs, "Let me go! I'm not Bona!"

"Don't scream. If you scream, they might come. And I'd rather kill you myself than allow you to fall alive into their hands."

Between Elvina and the ladder there was this boy. He had picked up a second lamp from the ground. He spoke to Elvina as one speaks to a child, slowly and rather tenderly. "I understand, Bona, I understand. You hid under a false name. It was the right thing to do. But with me you are safe. You see, I have a knife. No one can do you any harm. No one knows I have a key to this cellar. You will remain here, in perfect safety."

The boy's tunic was very dirty, belted with a thick cord from which hung a long butcher's knife. The boy kept running his finger along the blade, as if to make sure it was well-sharpened. Elvina was struggling to hide how terrified she was. She had to convince this boy with the wild eyes to let her go!

"What's your name? she asked.

The boy looked at her sternly. "We are alone, Bona. You no longer have to pretend not to recognize me. I'm Ephraim ben Isaac ben Judah ben Meshullam, your twin brother who has always loved you and protected you."

Columba's words came back to Elvina, "My cousins, Bona and Matriona . . . Bona looked like you . . ." So, this Ephraim was Columba's cousin. Elvina's courage returned. This boy was not an unknown person. There had to be a way of reasoning with him. Resolutely, she turned her eyes away from the knife and asked, taking pains to control the trembling in her voice, "Do you use this mirror?"

If he bends down to pick up the mirror, I'll make a dash for the ladder, she thought. But Ephraim's thinking was quicker than hers. He grabbed her wrist. He was much too strong for her even to try pulling away. He did not let go of her until he had the mirror in his other hand. Then, as if nothing had happened, he explained, "Our master Simeon bar Isaac the Great, who lived in our city of Mainz, owned several mirrors. In them he could see the events that had already taken place, and those that would take place. I only have one mirror. In it I see what has already taken place." He sounded angry now and his eyes had clouded over.

"What do you see in your mirror?" What a cruel, useless question! Elvina was immediately sorry she had asked. She already knew what the wild-eyed boy saw in his mirror. Quickly, she added, "No, you don't need to tell me. Let's speak about something else. Please, Ephraim, I don't want to know the past."

But Ephraim had grasped the mirror. He brought it very close to his face, and, swaying as if reciting a passage from the Talmud, he started to chant. "Ephraim's grandfather is wrapped up in his prayer shawl. The prayer shawl is covered with blood. The synagogue is burning. The Torah scrolls are burning. The flames of the sacrifice are ascending toward the skies. Perhaps they are agreeable to the Almighty, who knows? Ephraim sees his father and his mother, he sees his sisters and his little brother, he hears his mother calling out to him and he doesn't answer. He is crawling, he wants to escape. He hears the rough words of the Crusaders, and his mother's voice calling him. But he is hidden, flattened out under a chest. There is blood all around him."

The hand holding the mirror dropped. Ephraim looked at Elvina. Elvina was sobbing. She managed to calm down and dried her eyes with her sleeve.

"Ephraim, let me go," she cried. "I'll come back very soon. I promise."

Chapter

31

Several times Elvina repeated her promise to return very soon. Ephraim didn't look at her. Maybe he didn't hear her. He just dropped onto his straw mattress and once again started scrutinizing the surface of his mirror, swaying a little, as if he were studying. He didn't even seem to notice when the girl he called Bona turned away, walked to the ladder, and climbed up.

As she was coming out of the trapdoor, Elvina found herself face to face with Columba. Columba jumped back and let out a scream. "Is he there?" she gasped.

"You mean your cousin Ephraim? He's there. I just met him. He thinks I'm his twin sister."

Columba stared at Elvina, and Elvina stared back. Columba's face seemed to have suddenly shriveled up like the face of an old woman. "Now you know," she whispered.

"What do I know?"

"That my cousin's family was massacred by the Crusaders and that my unfortunate cousin has gone . . ." Columba looked all around to check that no one was listening. Who in the world could be listening, Elvina wondered, since the street is deserted? Finally, in a hoarse whisper, Columba let out the word: "Mad!"

"Why is he being left in the cellar?" Elvina asked.

"He jumped down into it the moment we arrived here. When my parents tried to come near him, he insulted them and threatened them with his knife. He makes them feel ashamed that they're still alive when his own parents have died. I'm the only one he doesn't threaten, so I'm in charge of bringing him food. I'm also the only one who knows he has a key and sometimes wanders about at night. He made me swear not to tell anyone."

"Why didn't your father mention Ephraim to my grandfather?"

"He's ashamed. Ephraim reminds my parents of what they now

117

consider to have been an act of cowardice. To have agreed to let us all be baptized so that we would not die."

Elvina stroked her friend's hair.

"Poor Columba. And that egg you were looking for, the egg that had to be newly laid by a black hen, that was for Ephraim, not for Godolias, am I right?"

"Yes. And it has to be the hen's very first egg," Columba admitted. "My grandfather left us a notebook that contains hundreds of recipes. There are several for restoring a person's memory, opening his heart, and removing the stone that blocks it and makes it heavy. I'm desperate to find something that will bring relief to Ephraim and set his heart free. I want him to start studying again instead of spending his time gazing into his mirror to watch his parents die over and over again, or copying verses, always the same ones, that tell of owls invading houses."

Columba's dark eyes were brimming with tears, and the tears had started to roll down her cheeks. "If you only knew what he was like before! He was by far the most brilliant and the most learned of all the boys of our community. And the most pious, too! And so affectionate with his sisters and even with me, his cousin. Now, I'm not even sure he recognizes me."

"What about the egg? Did you find it?" Elvina was curious.

Columba shook her head. "No. I don't dare search for it anymore. You heard that farm woman accusing me of sorcery!"

"I might be able to get you an egg! But show me the recipe!"

"Hide in the doorway so no one will see you and wait for me."

Columba was back in no time. She brought a notebook made of sheets of parchment sewn together with coarse thread. The parchment was thick and a little greasy, the pages dirty and covered with writing, even in the corners. There was hardly any space between the lines, so that they sometimes overlapped. There were no margins, no borders of any kind. "You're able to read from this book?" asked Elvina with disbelief.

"If you look closely, you'll see that it's a common square handwriting. There's nothing unusual about it for a person who is accustomed to read the sacred language. The words are easy. It's just that the writing is very small and cramped."

Columba opened the notebook, turned several pages, and showed the place with her finger. Together they read, "Prince of the Torah, who stood with Moses at Mount Sinai and crowned him, nourish me with all that he learned and that his ears heard, and remove the stone that is burdening my heart without delay. Amen."

"Now the book tells you what to do." Columba pointed to the words. "Read."

Elvina read, "Write this sentence on the shell of an egg freshly laid by a black hen, then roast the egg. Then remove the shell. Then write these words again on the egg itself. Then eat it. Do not eat or drink anything else on that day."

"There is another recipe that says you must boil the egg," added Columba.

"Can you write small enough to fit that whole sentence on the egg? By the way, this recipe does not call for the black hen's first egg!"

"That comes from another recipe," answered Columba, a little sheepishly.

"You're mixing different recipes?"

"I want to put all the chances on my side, you understand?" Columba seemed to be appealing to Elvina. She looked so sad that Elvina threw her arms around her friend and hugged her. "I'll help you. I'll find the egg. And . . . I have some other ideas."

"What other ideas? You're not planning to give away our secret, are you?" Columba panicked.

"No. But I've heard the apothecary praise the effectiveness of the madder plant in the treatment of melancholy. I'll buy some from him under a false pretext and he'll explain to me how to use it. I also have another idea. We'll see if it helps cure your cousin."

Just as she was leaving, Elvina remembered Godolias. "What about your little brother? Is he in good health?" she asked Columba.

"My mother is taking care of him. He'll go back to school tomorrow."

"He's the reason I came here today. I wanted to inquire about him! Little did I expect . . . !"

Columba kissed Elvina good-bye.

Now Elvina walked fast. Go, girl, go, she thought, don't waste any time! One of our brothers must be saved. A young life must start again, where it has been broken, just as a tree throws out a new shoot from the very branch that was cut. So go, girl, hurry, you'll cure this Ephraim, you'll pull him out of his madness, he will study with Solomon ben Isaac and some day, who knows, he might even be a husband worthy of sweet Fleurdelys.

Elvina laughed at herself. So you've become a matchmaker! You're not even married. What would your grandfather say?

Elvina came to a sudden halt. Yes, what would Solomon ben Isaac say? Two women returning from the well, a heavy pail of water in each hand, glanced at Elvina with a mixture of surprise and curiosity. Elvina nodded, they nodded, too, and one of them smiled. What would they say if they knew that a mad boy was hiding in their neighborhood? Of course, Elvina thought to herself, if your grandfather were here in town, you would rush and tell him about Ephraim. You would not undertake to nurse a young madman. But at this very moment Solomon ben Isaac is peacefully riding toward Châlons, may the Almighty protect him. If, during his absence, the neighborhood should learn about Ephraim . . . Better not to think of what might happen. Ephraim might be mistreated, even beaten. Chased away from Troyes. He would go and die in the forest. Judah ben Nathan, of course, is home, but he feels no sympathy at all for the German family. What about Obadiah? Obadiah? He would have to submit to Judah ben Nathan's decision. So, girl, keep the secret of Ephraim until the return of Solomon ben Isaac. But just until his return and not one instant longer, Elvina reassured herself.

As always, the apothecary was delighted to see Elvina. "Elvina! To what do I owe the pleasure?"

Before she could explain what she wanted, the apothecary resumed speaking. "I see you didn't bring your little protégée with you this morning. I prefer that and I won't pretend to the contrary. You only listen to your kind heart, Elvina, we all know that, you take after your grandfather, Master Solomon. But you see, people are scared now. Ever since the German family came here things have been happening. Strange parchments with frightening messages are raining on the town. Children are being devoured by the red fever. Animals have been slaughtered. Did you know a puppy was found dead earlier this morning? You didn't know? Well, let's stop talking about disagreeable topics. Your visit is such a pleasure for me. Did Mistress Miriam, your mother, send you?"

The apothecary rose from his stool without putting down his mortar and pestle. His red beard was truly enormous.

"See this lovely powder," he showed her what was in his mortar. "Aniseed, horseradish, muscat flower, cardamom, dill, parsley, and chicory. You crush it all up, mix it with wine, and it performs miracles! It's especially miraculous for kidney ailments. Oh, and I almost forgot the most important part: you have to drink it just after the new moon!"

Elvina hoped her eyes had not betrayed the fact that she hadn't listened to a word he was saying. Her heart was pounding madly and when she spoke she had to make a real effort to keep her voice steady. "I remember you once explained to me the properties of the madder plant."

"Yes, the madder plant is an excellent remedy for melancholy. You tie the stems into knots, then you attach the whole thing to the neck of the person afflicted with melancholy, which is a fancy name for a sadness that won't go away. It is in the Talmud. Ask your father. Ask your mother, she knows this as well as I do."

"My mother is too busy right now. She is nursing the sick children."

The apothecary bowed and smiled. Elvina took a deep breath. She was about to tell a lie, a brazen lie. "I was wondering if a few knots of madder could bring relief to my cousin Samuel, who has been sad since his parents went back to Ramerupt."

She wasn't risking much. Samuel never spoke to the apothecary. He only saw him at the synagogue on the Sabbath, and by that time . . .

The apothecary didn't suspect anything. He replied very cheerfully, "That's precisely the usage recommended in the Talmud by Rabbi . . . uhh . . . You'll forgive me, I'm not a very learned man. But what I can tell you is that my madder comes directly from Spain. Look at these pretty yellow flowers and the strong leaves growing all around the stem. Here, take a nice bunch. You'll pay me later. Your cousin Samuel ben Meir is already a great scholar so take good care of him!"

When Elvina got home, she found Gauthier's horse standing in the courtyard.

Chapter 32

Zipporah was squatting in front of her boiling soup and watching Gauthier's horse with obvious and intense dislike. The horse didn't pay any attention to the old servant, being much too preoccupied with his own fatigue, the fatigue of a horse who has just galloped for a long while. He snorted, his head hung low. He was covered with sweat; Gauthier must have pressed him hard!

"Our pretty young knight has returned," Zipporah yelled out as soon as she saw Elvina. "He's asking for your grandfather. If you want my opinion, this is only a pretext. You're the one he's after!"

"Elvina!"

The joyful expression on Gauthier's face as he came out of Solomon ben Isaac's door seemed to confirm Zipporah's opinion. Elvina walked toward him. "You're looking for my grandfather, I'm told."

"Yes. I decided to gather up my courage and beg him to allow me to sit in on a few of his lessons. The monks gave me permission to spend a whole week sitting at the feet of Solomon ben Isaac!"

"You've chosen the wrong week! Solomon ben Isaac is in Châlons. We hope to see him back for the Sabbath."

Gauthier seemed sincerely disappointed, which went against Zipporah's opinion. The horse had recognized his master's voice and whinnied softly, then he let out a few snorts that meant he was hungry and thirsty. Gauthier went up to him and patted his nostrils. "You'll eat when you're not so hot any more. Perhaps our friend Elvina will bring me a cloth to wipe you down with," he said affectionately to the horse. Then he turned to Elvina. "To make up for this, just a little, could you give me a lesson, and also some more reading material?"

Elvina couldn't help laughing. There was something in Gauthier's smile, in Gauthier's eyes, that made it impossible to refuse him. "Yes," she agreed, "a short lesson. And some exercises in reading our sacred language. If you want, you may stay here for the midday meal.

122

Zipporah is preparing a delicious soup, and you can enjoy the pleasure of a discussion with Samuel. He and Yom Tov should be here any moment, now."

It was Gauthier's turn to laugh. "Is it possible that the pleasure I take in having discussions with your cousin irks you? But I like talking with you, too, as you very well know. What are you reading, these days?"

"The psalms. I read them and learn them by heart. And I copy my favorite ones into my personal notebook."

"Could you help me read some?"

"They're too difficult. You're just a beginner, may I remind you!"

"And I'll remind you that I happen to know the psalms by heart in Latin!"

"We'll see."

Elvina hurried into the house and came back with a cloth. As Gauthier started to wipe down his horse, Elvina was struck by a wonderful idea. "Gauthier, listen to me, I need your help!"

She looked so serious that Gauthier straightened up immediately. He stood very tall in front of her, looking extremely grave, brave, and ready for anything. "You only have to ask," he said. "You know I will never forget how much I owe you."

"Do you remember the two girls who were on the river bank when the horseman threatened me and you intervened?"

"Yes."

"Their names are Jeanne and Marguerite. They are Christians, like you."

Gauthier frowned. "Am I supposed to care? Those two girls are of no interest to me!"

"Their parents raise hens. Nobody in all of Troyes owns as many hens as they do. And I, well, I need an egg."

Gauthier looked as if he couldn't believe his ears. "You need an egg? Well, ask them for an egg! Surely they won't refuse you!"

He went back to his horse again, but Elvina insisted, "I don't need just any egg. I need an egg laid by a black hen and it has to be the hen's first egg."

Gauthier abruptly stopped what he was doing. He turned to stare at Elvina, then he frowned. "I'm beginning to understand," he said. "You're afraid they will accuse you of witchcraft! But allow me to say that, in this case, well, their suspicions might be . . . forgive me . . . but they might . . . for someone who didn't know you very well . . . they might appear . . . justified!"

Elvina's heart was pounding madly. She spoke fast. "Listen to me. There is no sorcery involved. Do you remember what Yom Tov told you the other day? That eggs are good for the memory?"

"Yes."

"This is just a recipe for restoring the memory of an unfortunate boy who has lost it. An ordinary egg would not be potent enough, so we need an egg that is a little out of the ordinary. Only I cannot ask Christians. They would immediately suspect me of the worst practices. Whereas you . . . They'll be so thrilled, so honored to receive your visit!"

"But how am I supposed to justify such a strange request?"

"Explain that it is a recipe you got from the monks, or some kind of curiosity on your part, tell them you read in a book that such an egg had an incomparable flavor. What you say is of no importance. Coming from you, it will just seem like a very amusing and charming whim because you are above suspicion and no one will ever accuse you of doing sorcery!"

Gauthier laughed.

"You've got it all figured out. But tell me about the boy who lost his memory."

"Promise you will keep my secret."

Gauthier bowed. "I give you my word of honor. That's the very least I owe you."

"I want to try and cure a boy who has gone mad. An orphan exactly our age. He comes from Mainz. He saw his whole family being massacred."

"By the Crusaders?"

Elvina nodded yes. Both remained silent for a long while. Gauthier had become very pale. "If they had accepted baptism, they would be alive," he finally said. "But still, I'm telling this to you, I'm ashamed. I'm ashamed that my brothers have killed people who did no harm, who were neither armed nor dangerous, respectable people like . . ."

He stopped short and his face went from white to bright red.

"You mean people like my grandfather? Like my parents? Like me? That's what you were about to say?" Elvina asked.

"Yes. I often think about our first conversation. You said to me: 'Your Jesus spoke our language.' I answered you that I already knew this. I knew it, yes, but before meeting you I had never really thought about it. I had never thought about the fact that Jesus was a Jew. But tell me about this boy."

"He's in hiding. As you were, last year. And he has gone mad. He doesn't study. He never stops seeing the death of his father, of his mother, of his sisters and his brother. He thinks I'm one of his sisters, a girl named Bona, who is dead. It breaks my heart. If you saw him, you would feel a great pity, I assure you."

"And you think you can cure him?"

"I'm going to try. I have several ideas."

"Tell me where the house of Marguerite and Jeanne is. I'll run there right now! I'll go back as often as necessary—two, three times a day—until the infamous black hen lays her first egg. And this first egg shall be brought to you. You have Gauthier's word of honor!"

Elvina burst out laughing.

"To reward you for your zeal, I'll read several passages from the Bible with you this afternoon, and I'll copy a few more pages for you to keep. But I think you should eat with Yom Tov and Samuel before going on the egg quest."

Gauthier thanked her. Then he asked, "Is this how you look at Obadiah? Is this how you smile at him? If it is, then I don't know what he's waiting for to marry you!"

"Who said I was marrying him?"

"No one. I thought . . ."

"You'd do a lot better to tend to your horse! He's starving!"

Chapter
33

When she reached Dieulesault's house, Elvina stopped and waited for two men who were walking behind her to pass. They were probably on their way to the synagogue. They would think she was visiting Matriona, Dieulesault's daughter, and their curiosity would not be aroused.

As soon as the men turned the corner, she walked on to Columba's house. She made sure there was no one on the street, squatted down by the trapdoor, and knocked lightly a few times.

She heard the ladder steps squeaking. Someone was climbing up. "Open up, Ephraim, it's me," she whispered.

"Bona?"

Elvina barely paused before answering. "Yes, it's me, Bona."

The trapdoor opened. Ephraim climbed back down the steps. Elvina followed him. The first thing she saw was the gleam of the knife hanging from his belt. For an instant, she hesitated. The small voice she knew so well was practically yelling, "You reckless girl! You're courting disaster!" "Quiet!" she replied silently. "I'm his sister, remember? He wishes me no harm. I must help him!" Then she took a deep breath, went down the last step, and smiled at the tall thin boy. "I see that you have eaten. Columba brought you some oatmeal. It's good, isn't it? I, too, have brought you several things."

He didn't answer. From her sleeve, she drew a small flask. She opened it and handed it to Ephraim. "Drink! It's the water left over from bread dough that was kneaded this morning. It's refreshing and will do you good. It's recommended for those who study."

The boy took the flask. He examined it with distrust. He brought it up to his lips but didn't drink, then he moved it away from his mouth, looked at it again, brought it back, moved it away, back and forth . . . until Elvina cried out, "It's only water, water that will do you good! Drink! I order you to drink it!"

In a flash, Ephraim opened his mouth and poured in the contents of the flask.

"Good," approved Elvina. "You'll drink some of that every day."

She slid the flask back into her right sleeve. Then, from her left sleeve, she took the madder plant. She knotted the stems carefully following the apothecary's instructions and added a long lace to make it stronger and easier to attach.

"You are going to let me tie this around your neck. You won't feel anything; it's very light. This plant will protect you, it will protect us. I am going to wear some, too."

While she spoke, she tied the madder plant around Ephraim's neck, using the lace. He allowed her to do this, but not once did his eyes rest on the girl who was adorning him with such a strange necklace. He didn't even seem to be aware of her presence. His eyes were dull.

"Ephraim," Elvina now said to him, "I've brought you a second mirror, a mirror in which you will be able to read the future. The one you have only shows events that have already taken place."

From her sleeve, Elvina took out the mirror her aunt Yochebed had given to her. She showed it to Ephraim. "Take this mirror. It's for you. It's a mirror that tells the future. This way, you'll have both the past and the future—just like Rabbi Simeon bar Isaac the Great."

Ephraim took the mirror, but he didn't look at it. He was standing in front of Elvina, staring vacantly into the distance. So Elvina decided to jump in. She said, "Ephraim, look into the mirror, the mirror that predicts the future."

Ephraim didn't seem to hear her. She repeated, "Please! Look at the mirror!"

Ephraim bent over his pile of clothes, picked up the other mirror, gazed at its surface, and just as he had done the day before began to chant. "The Crusaders are throwing the Torah scrolls on the ground and trampling them. Ephraim is hiding under the chest; blood is flowing on the ground, toward Ephraim. He hears his mother's voice calling him . . ."

"Enough, Ephraim!" Elvina couldn't stand it any more. "Look at the other mirror, the mirror of the future, look into it, I am begging you, your sister Bona is begging you!"

Ephraim shrugged his shoulders. But he raised the other mirror up to his eyes. A long moment went by. Ephraim's face was expression-less.

"What do you see?" Elvina murmured.

He didn't answer. She came near him. She too gazed at the surface of the mirror. In it she saw Ephraim's face, his mop of black hair and one of her own braids. She avoided meeting the boy's eyes. She backed away a little, allowed some time to go by, then again she asked him, "What do you see?"

A kind of hoarse breathing was her answer. She thought she made out the word "Nothing."

She moved closer to him once more. "Do you want to know what I see?"

No answer. Elvina decided to continue. "I see an orphaned boy who is suffering, and I see my grandfather, Solomon ben Isaac, taking this boy in his arms and comforting him. I see Solomon ben Isaac blessing this boy as he would a beloved son, placing his hand on his head, very gently, and I see the boy beginning to study again."

Ephraim's only response was to throw Elvina's mirror on his straw mattress. He picked up the mirror of the past again and, his voice full of rage, started to chant: "Ephraim's grandfather is sitting with the other sages and teachers of the community. They are sitting, wrapped up in their prayer shawls, in the archbishop's courtyard. The archbishop promised to protect them but did not protect them. The prayer shawls are soaked in blood. The most pious and most erudite Kalonymos ben Meshullam, father of Ephraim's mother, is dead. Ephraim's grandfather no longer exists."

Elvina was shaking. She started to cry from pity and also because she felt discouraged. But she wouldn't give up. "Ephraim, for the love of me, please continue to look into the mirror of the future. I assure you there is another grandfather, a grandfather who is also a great teacher. He is old but still walks with steady steps. His name is Solomon ben Isaac. One day you will see him, he will be coming toward you with outstretched arms and you will see his eyes resting on you, eyes filled with love and kindness. You will see the orphan Ephraim go to him and throw himself into his arms. You will see all that in the mirror of the future."

Then she moved away and Ephraim did not attempt to detain her. When she reached the top of the ladder, Elvina turned around and got a last glimpse of him, sitting on his mattress, a mirror in each hand, not looking at either of them.

Outside, Columba was waiting. "Well?"

Elvina sighed. "Take this little bag. Boil the leaves for a long time in milk and try to make your cousin drink some tonight. He must sleep. My mother and grandmother always give teas and potions to induce sleep in those who are tormented."

"What about my egg?"

Elvina smiled. "You'll have it! Gauthier is going to find it."

"Gauthier?"

"Oh! I was forgetting! You don't know him, He is a knight who is at my service. I'll see you tomorrow, Columba!"

Chapter 34

Now, Mazal, dear Mazal, you must admit I was right to go down into that cellar! I heard you saying that I was being terribly reckless. But if you only knew the pity I feel for poor unhappy Ephraim! I so badly want him to be cured! I intend to hide him until my grandfather returns because only Solomon ben Isaac can protect him. Three more days to wait!

If only time would move a little faster! I'm not at all certain that I've been of any real help to Ephraim. Night and day I fear a new outburst of his madness. I spend most of my time searching for ways to cure him. Columba and I are feverishly reading her recipe book, but we have to hide and pretend we are looking at embroidery patterns since we can only meet on the street!

Gauthier found an excellent pretext for going every day to Master Hubert's farm: he stabled his horse there for the duration of his stay in Troyes. So, every morning, he goes there to pat and stroke the dear thing. What could be more natural? And today, today . . . He walked into our courtyard and told Zipporah he was looking for Samuel. I came out to speak with him, and he handed me a small package: the egg!

Gauthier was laughing. "Finally! It was high time that black hen gave us her first egg!"

"I was afraid it would take much longer," I answered. "Perhaps it's a good omen. For Ephraim, I mean, for his recovery."

"I hope so. I'm also very happy for my own sake."

"For your own sake? What do you mean?"

"You're not the one who has to endure Master Hubert's teasing every morning as he escorts me to the stable. 'I know our young knight is still waiting for his egg!' he says. 'Hens, eggs, they're the business of women! You need to go see them!' And then he pushes me all the way to the house, where I have no choice but to make myself amiable to your friends, Marguerite and Jeanne, and their little sister, Marie, who gazes at me every time as if I were some kind of miraculous vision . . . The two older girls are always teasing me about this fanciful wish of mine to eat the first egg of a black hen . . . And the father of course is convinced I'm only interested in his daughters, whereas I can assure you I feel nothing of the kind. But now, finally, it's over!"

Gauthier smiled mischievously before going on. "Tomorrow I will announce to them that the egg was delicious, that never in my life have I tasted an egg whose flavor was remotely comparable. And that will be that."

I couldn't wait to bring the egg over to Columba's, but Gauthier's report was so entertaining that I was in no rush to hear him finish. He has such a way of telling a story! And when I look into his eyes I remember my little cousin Fleurdelys, who saw the reflection of the sky in them.

Needless to say, Zipporah never took her angry eyes off us during the whole conversation.

When Gauthier went off to find Samuel, I ran to Columba's. I asked her how she proposed to write the entire sentence on the egg shell.

"Don't worry! My handwriting is extremely small, and besides, if the letters overlap a little, it doesn't matter." She laughed almost soundlessly, a very pretty laugh. It was the first time I heard her laugh.

While Columba went back into her house to write the sentence on the egg and then roast it, I went down to the cellar to see Ephraim. He still had the madder necklace around his neck. And the knife was still hanging from his belt.

He was squatting on the ground, busy covering with verses the few margins he had left. He was writing from memory. He obviously knows the psalms and the book of Isaiah by heart. I told him I admired his beautiful handwriting. He didn't answer. He took one of the parchment strips and chanted the words of the prophet as if he were in the synagogue: "Behold, the Lord will lay waste the earth and make it desolate, he will turn it upside down and scatter its inhabitants." He put down the parchment, picked up another one, and again started chanting, his eyes staring far off into the distance: "Your enemies rage, Your foes lift up their heads."

I told him I knew this verse, which comes from a psalm. I told him that, when I have time, I copy psalms in order to have my own book. Ephraim frowned as he listened to me, and then all of a sudden his face lit up. He smiled at me, a radiant and tender smile such as I had never seen on a boy's face. "I remember. You've always loved writing, Bona! When we were little, you mastered the art of writing long before I did!"

And I thought that Bona was dead and Ephraim was smiling for nothing. I started to cry. Ephraim seemed surprised, but he didn't say anything more.

That's when Columba arrived. She showed us the roasted egg, which was completely covered with tiny letters. Then, carefully and without hurrying, she peeled off the shell. I admired the daintiness of her fingers and the precision of her gestures. I'm not nearly that skillful! Then, using her fingernail, she wrote the characters on the white of the egg, slowly turning the egg between her fingers. The whole cellar echoed with her lovely flutelike voice. "Prince of the Torah, who stood with Moses at Mount Sinai and crowned him, nourish me with all that he learned and that his ears heard, and remove the stone that is burdening my heart without delay."

Ephraim obediently ate the egg without uttering a word. The two mirrors were resting on his mattress, as on the previous days. For a moment, I thought of picking them up and trying to encourage Ephraim to consult them with me. But he had seen my eyes moving. When he feels a danger, he is very quick. He flung himself between the mattress and me, and declared, "No one touches these mirrors. They belong to me. They are the mirror of the past and the mirror of the future."

I stood up in front of him and said, "Please look into the mirror of the future."

But he picked up the mirror of the past. And, again, he chanted, "I see Ephraim studying with his grandfather, Kalonymos ben Meshullam, I see the Crusaders pouring into the streets of the city like a boiling river, I see the swords sparkling in the sun and then the sun itself becoming dark, I see flames going up toward the sky, consuming the synagogue and the Torah scrolls. The prayer shawls are soaked in blood . . ."

"Stop!"

Columba was clinging to her cousin's arm. She was shaking him. "I beg you, Ephraim, stop looking into that mirror! It only hurts you!"

He very gently made her let go and went to lie down, still holding his two mirrors, one in each hand.

That was today. Tomorrow we'll try another recipe. Yes, Mazal, I know you find me very stubborn. But I would despise myself if I didn't try everything I can think of to cure Ephraim.

Chapter 35

Never had time moved so slowly, yet never had Elvina been so busy. Every day she prepared potions and ointments for Precious and Miriam, for the sick children, who were all recovering, thank God. Every day Elvina copied passages from the sacred texts onto her wax tablets and read them with Gauthier, under the watchful eye of Zipporah, who did not wish Gauthier well. Every day she listened to Samuel and Yom Tov reciting and chanting the Mishnah they were studying that day, and she tried to remember as much of it as she could. Every day she served the boys their midday meal and heard Samuel argue with Gauthier.

But every day, she was only waiting for the time to come when she could run and meet Columba and consult the recipe book with her. Every day, all she really thought about was the moment when she would climb down the ladder to Ephraim's cellar. Every day she dreaded to hear that another animal had been found in the neighborhood with its throat slit.

There was no time to go to the school. The low stool was waiting for her in vain. Elvina wondered whether Obadiah had noticed her absence.

Every day she made buns with the best wheat flour, honey, and nuts. Samuel and Yom Tov were delighted, and Judah ben Nathan even more!

"My daughter is becoming an accomplished housemistress," he began to say quite often. Had he only known the truth! Had he known that Elvina was baking all of these buns for the sole purpose of writing on one of them: "Remove the stone that is burdening my heart without delay. Amen."

Every day Ephraim swallowed his bun without seeming to pay any attention. His eyes were now shiny, now dull. Nothing changed.

One day, Columba poured wine into a goblet. "Here's a formula we haven't tried yet. We'll sit next to Ephraim and recite it together.

This is to make him forget the visions that are tormenting him and open up his heart so he can study once more."

She dipped her finger in the wine. Then, on the surface of the wine, she wrote the words while both girls recited: "I implore you, Potach, Prince of Forgetfulness, to remove from me this weak and foolish heart and throw it on a high mountain, in the name of the names Arimas, Arimimas, Ansisiel, and Petachiel . . ."

There was absolute silence in the cellar. Ephraim was looking at the wine goblet without displaying any emotion. On the light surface of the wine the trace of Columba's slender finger had vanished right away.

"The characters dissolved exactly as they were supposed to," Columba whispered. Then she handed the goblet to Elvina. "Here! You make him drink it! He obeys you!"

While Ephraim drank the wine, Elvina looked around, wondering where he had hidden the mirrors. She couldn't see them. She asked, "Ephraim, please look into the mirror of the future today, just for me, to please me."

Ephraim went to his mattress and unfolded his blanket. The two mirrors had been wrapped up in it. He took them both out.

"The mirror of the future, today," Elvina repeated. "Only the mirror of the future!"

Ephraim's face was frozen. His voice flat, resigned. "You know it's of no use, Bona!"

"Please, Ephraim, for my sake! Try!"

Ephraim repeated, "For your sake, Bona."

Elvina felt she was committing an act of horrible dishonesty. But perhaps some good might come of it.

Ephraim brought Elvina's mirror, the mirror of the future, up close to his eyes.

"What do you see?"

Ephraim was frowning. He peered intensely into the smooth surface of the mirror, but he remained silent. As she had done a few days before, Elvina came near him and she, too, scrutinized the surface of the mirror. She could see Ephraim's eyes. They were shining and yet seemed blind.

"Look hard!" she said. "You will see a table set for the Sabbath. You will see the Sabbath lamp, a pretty silver lamp that gives out a soft light. You will see the warmth and kindness in the eyes of the grandfather who sits at the head of the table. This grandfather's name is Solomon ben Isaac. He is reciting the blessing. Next to him sits the boy named Ephraim. Solomon ben Isaac has placed his arm around the boy's shoulders and holds him close, as a grandfather does with his favorite grandson."

"You are lying, Bona! There is no grandfather! No Sabbath lamp! No soft light!"

Ephraim grabbed the mirror of the past with both of his hands. He bent over it as if he were peering down into deep dark water, and he swayed and chanted, "The Sabbath has gone up in flames, the Torah scrolls have burned, the blood of the Jews is flowing, Ephraim is hiding . . ."

On that day, Elvina cried as she walked home. For the first time in her life, she felt she had committed an act of cruelty. And yet, when she tried to take away the mirror of the future from Ephraim he had refused to hand it to her.

Tomorrow, she thought, tomorrow, Grandfather is due to return. Finally! May the Almighty grant him a safe journey!

Chapter
36

"Polish the plates, child, rub the goblets and the Sabbath lamp until they shine and you see your face in them, then cover the table with our most beautiful white linen tablecloth. Tonight, after the service, Solomon ben Isaac is bringing back two guests from Spain, rich, educated merchants who are accustomed to every imaginable refinement!"

Thus spoke Precious who, since morning, had run her dust rag at least three times along places already cleaned by the servants, and with her broom had swept corners the servants had already swept clean. Honey cakes and compotes of dried figs and ginger were ready to be served, beautifully arranged on the family's very best silver plates.

The warm, sweet smell of bread rising and baking in the oven filled the house.

In the courtyard, Zipporah had a huge fire going. Several chickens were roasting. Later on when the flames died down a little, she would grill the fish. Solomon had often explained to Precious that Spanish Jews made fun of their northern brothers' meat stews, which they declared tasteless. They preferred their meat roasted or grilled.

Elvina was just as active and busy as everybody else: curiosity gave her wings. How many times had her grandfather praised to her the vast knowledge of the Spanish merchants "who read and write the language of Ishmael as well as our own sacred language, in addition to speaking the Romance language, which is the everyday language in Spain, just as we speak French, the language of our land of exile!"

She had to run to the spice merchant's to buy sage and thyme, which would give the fish a better flavor. When she returned, she was disappointed to hear that Solomon ben Isaac had arrived from Châlons and had set out for the synagogue after hastily washing and changing his clothes. But she didn't have the leisure to wonder when she might speak to him about Ephraim because already her grandmother was grabbing the spices right out of her hand. "Quick, Elvina! No one has put any oil in the lamps! Fill them up with good clean oil, and check the wicks, then go down to the cellar to draw some wine. Make sure we have plenty of pitchers!" She was all out of breath as if she had been the one running to the spice shop.

Late in the afternoon, a Spanish servant, draped in a broad cloak, brought several packages, which he silently put down on the table in front of Precious. Then he smiled, bowed very low, and left, as he had come, without a word.

At the last moment, when the table was set and everything was in place, Precious sent Elvina to her house. "Wash your hands and face, comb your hair, and put on your blue dress. And tell your mother to dress up a little. Bring her this wimple and this headscarf; they are clean and well starched."

Judah ben Nathan, who was just about to return to the synagogue, heard Elvina conveying the orders to Miriam. "Why all these preparations?" he grumbled disagreeably. "Nobody is getting married to my knowledge."

Miriam laughed. "True. But everybody knows the Spaniards are proud of their elegant ways and clothes. They consider themselves to be more civilized than we are, and they feel contempt for us."

"Grandmother is very eager for us to make a good impression. She doesn't want our Spanish brothers to return home and make it known that we, the Jews of Troyes, are ill-bred, slovenly boors," Elvina added.

Judah ben Nathan shrugged his shoulders. "We're better talmudists than they are, and no one would even dream of denying it!"

Elvina cast a sidelong glance at her father. "In any case, my father can't possibly see anything wrong with our desire to adorn ourselves to greet the Sabbath, can he?"

Judah ben Nathan threw up his arms and laughed. "What woman wants! Go on, deck yourselves out, but hurry! There's not much time left before sunset."

Later, when Solomon ben Isaac returned from the synagogue, accompanied by his guests, Elvina was waiting for them at the door. Judah ben Nathan walked with them. Obadiah, Samuel and Yom Tov followed. Elvina was rather pleased with her blue dress, which was almost new, as she had only worn it two or three times. It was the exact color of cornflowers, long and loose, pleated all the way down and gathered at the hips by a very thin belt embroidered by Miriam, which made the dress puff out just a tiny bit.

Obadiah walked toward her, deep in conversation with Samuel and Yom Tov. Elvina wished he would look at her, but she also wished he wouldn't. He did raise his head and his eyes rested on her just for a brief moment, then he resumed his conversation with the boys. But in his eyes Elvina had time to read something that made her feel beautiful in her cornflower dress. She smiled, to no one in particular.

The Sabbath lamp had been lit and Precious was standing at the head of the table. Quickly, Elvina kissed her grandfather to welcome him home. This was obviously not the time to mention Ephraim. She would do so first thing in the morning.

The Spanish merchant, Yakub ben Yussef, had brought his son Zakkariya with him. Zakkariya was about the same age as Obadiah, about the same height, and also very dark haired. But that's where the resemblance stopped. The young Spaniard's eyes seemed to be constantly laughing, his hair and beard were elegantly trimmed, his tunic was made of thick gray wool and had never been torn or mended. The edges were embroidered. He, like his father, wore a stylish cloak lined with fur. The father's cloak was gray, while the son's cloak was green.

Yakub ben Yussef complimented Precious on her sumptuously set table. She frowned and shook her head, as if she doubted the sincerity of the compliment. But Elvina could see her grandmother was, in fact, very pleased.

The guests were seated on either side of Solomon ben Isaac. Judah ben Nathan, Obadiah ben Moyses, Samuel, and Yom Tov sat across the table, facing them. Precious, Miriam, and Elvina waited on them, sitting down now and then to listen to the conversation. The men were commenting on the week's parashah, which told of the Almighty's commandments to the children of Israel. It was a reading that Elvina particularly liked and had often heard her grandfather explain. The discussion took place in the sacred language with, now and then, words in the Spanish tongue, or in the French language that was spoken in Troyes. With a little patience, they could all understand one another.

Once the Sabbath meal was finished, Solomon ben Isaac recited the blessing. Elvina noticed the sparkle in her grandfather's eyes. She nudged her mother with her elbow. Miriam nodded and smiled. Both knew exactly what Solomon was about to say.

"Master Yakub ben Yussef has traveled much. This is not the case with his humble brothers of Troyes. Gladden our hearts with some accounts of your travels. Tell us about the things you have seen."

Yakub ben Yussef bowed. "First allow me to present you with the gifts my servant brought here this afternoon."

He handed Elvina's grandfather a package. Solomon unraveled the cloth, revealing a magnificent little chest made of light wood, inlaid all over with tiny pieces of an even lighter material, so pale as to be the color of cream.

"What a magnificent piece of work!"

Yakub, whose eyes had never left his host's face, saw that Solomon was sincerely enthusiastic. He laughed with pleasure. "I am happy this small chest finds favor in your eyes! It is made of sandalwood, and the inlays are ivory. Ivory comes from the long teeth of an elephant."

"Master Yakub has seen elephants?" Yom Tov couldn't restrain himself from crying out. Now, flushed with shame, he stared down at his plate.

Yakub burst out laughing. "Don't be embarrassed, my son! I do believe Master Solomon ben Isaac, your grandfather, was just about to ask the very same question."

Solomon laughed, too, and nodded.

The guest seemed delighted to have a chance to tell his stories.

"Indeed, I have seen elephants. They are huge beasts, capable of transporting a dozen men on their back. Their skin is the color of ashes and it is all wrinkled. Their legs resemble the branches of an old beech tree. And they have two curved teeth, which are several cubits long."

Everyone around the table was silent. Elvina tried to imagine an elephant. She thought she would be terrified if she ever saw one!

Solomon thanked Yakub. "I shall cherish this chest and take good care of it. I intend to keep my chess pieces in it."

Yakub smiled mischievously. "That's what it was built for. I have been told that Solomon ben Isaac enjoys a game of chess and often wins. I hope he will not disdain to play a game with me tomorrow afternoon. We shall dispose our queens, our kings, and our horsemen in battle array! A peaceful battle since it is a battle of cleverness, during which neither sword nor dagger is to be unsheathed!"

"How beautifully he speaks!" Elvina whispered in her mother's ear.

"Our Spanish brothers are accustomed to keep company with the nobles of their country. They are knowledgeable in poetry as well as in music. It is true that, in some respects, we are peasants compared to them," replied Miriam, also whispering.

But Yakub ben Yussef was not finished. He held several smaller packages in his hands. "Will Master Solomon allow me to present a few gifts to his wife and to his daughter and granddaughter?"

Solomon bowed.

All watched as Precious, then Miriam, unwrapped lovely embroidered belts. Finally, Yakub handed Miriam a very light package. "Unless I am much mistaken, it will not be long before the young lady I see sitting next to you will be married. I make bold to hope she will wear my present, on holidays, for her pleasure and that of her husband."

If Obadiah smiles or even dares to look at me, I will never speak to him again as long as I live, thought Elvina.

From the corner of her eye, she saw that Obadiah was not smiling. His face was turned toward Yakub ben Yussef as if he were only waiting for the conversation to continue.

Together Elvina and her mother opened the linen envelope and Elvina took out a headscarf the like of which she had never seen. It was made of a thin, soft, shiny material that was incredibly supple and light, of the most beautiful red with gold embroidery all around the edges.

"Silk! This is a gift worthy of a queen!" Miriam exclaimed.

Yakub smiled. "You flatter me. Indeed it is silk, but I'm sure you know that silk is more common in our country than in yours."

The first thing Elvina thought was that she would never dare to put on such a headscarf. She had no idea what to say to this stranger who spoke so well and had just given her a veil worthy of a queen! She was very relieved when her grandfather took it upon himself to thank their guest.

"Master Yakub, you will forgive my granddaughter as she is not accustomed to receive such rich presents, and so I thank you on her behalf. And now, if you will, tell us about your travels. I have heard that you have crossed the Great Sea and journeyed to the Holy Land."

"Twice."

"Have you seen mermaids?"

"Yes, several times," Zakkariya answered. But Yakub ben Yussef shook his head. "From afar, my son, we saw them from afar. As soon as our ship approached them, they plunged into the water and we only saw their tails. You mustn't give our hosts a false impression."

But his son insisted. "Before they dove in, we caught a very clear glimpse of them."

It was Obadiah's turn to enquire. "Do they nurse their little ones?"

All eyes were on Zakkariya as he answered with great self-assurance, "Yes, of course."

His father was laughing. "My son has better eyesight than I do! They kept themselves at a considerable distance from us!"

Samuel, Yom Tov, and even Obadiah were gazing at the Spanish travelers with a combination of rapture and envy. These men had seen mermaids! They had seen, with their own eyes, the creatures mentioned in the Talmud, those hybrid beings, half human, half fish, born of relations between humans and dolphins!

Then they went on to talk about other wondrous sights, the streets of Jerusalem, gold-colored under the desert light, Mount Ararat, where a piece of Noah's Ark was still to be seen, and regions where manna, a white and terribly sweet substance, still fell. They spoke of Mesopotamia and of Syria. They spoke of Spain and the life that the Jews led there, which was so different from the life they knew in Troyes.

It was already late in the evening, but Solomon ben Isaac never tired of listening. He sat leaning toward his guests, his eyes shining, his hands resting in front of him on the table, his features relaxed and happy. He was so passionately interested in learning what one sees and smells in those distant countries where he would never travel!

Finally Zakkariya announced that he wished to recite a poem in honor of the young lady who would soon be married. It was a poem written in the sacred language by a great Jewish poet who had lived in Spain.

Elvina had not expected anything like that! She felt herself turning red, she wished she could disappear. She heard her father's dry cough. He was angry, to be sure! She didn't dare look at him. She threw a desperate glance at her grandfather and saw him frown but then immediately control himself and smile at Zakkariya. "It is not our custom, but for once, we will follow the custom of our guests."

Elvina almost screamed from the pain, so violently had her mother dug her elbow into her ribs. Miriam had straightened up. She smiled at Zakkariya. Her whole attitude was saying: Do as I do, child, take a hold on yourself, listen to the poem and thank the young man, don't give him the impression that our daughters are only capable of milking cows!

Zakkariya stood up, smiled all around him, explained that he had chosen the poem because it was inspired by the beautiful month of Iyyar, and began to recite. Elvina was much too embarrassed to be able to grasp the first lines. They seemed to be about a young man who gives his beloved some wine to drink, then prepares for her a bed of lilies and roses. Zakkariya didn't pronounce the sacred language quite as it was pronounced in Troyes, but Elvina could understand most of the words. "The beloved sleeps until morning. A peacock wakes her up. The peacock is standing in the middle of a garden and speaks to the flower bed, saying, 'Iyyar has adorned you like a king, and so you are like me, covered in embroidery, Iyyar has covered us both in azure, purple, and crimson!'"

Zakkariya's voice was sweet and musical. Never had Elvina heard anything like it. She was overcome, as by a lullaby, lulled by the music of the words so prettily arranged, the sounds returning just at the moment when one craved their return.

When Zakkariya's recitation came to an end, Elvina felt as if a very beautiful light had abruptly gone out and the air had become cold. She hid her face in her hands, hid that she felt like crying, hid that she wished, yes, she wished that Zakkariya would go on reciting.

But Solomon ben Isaac had risen from his seat. "It is high time we allowed our guests to take some rest."

Chapter 37

Deep in her sleep, Elvina heard a voice, then another. In her dream someone said, "They are singing once more in Solomon ben Isaac's house. Get up, Elvina. Hurry, go hear this voice, this song that delighted you so . . ."

But no, the voice reaching her in her sleep was not a song, it was a scream, soon followed by another scream, and another . . .

Elvina sat up. She was wide awake now. She heard her grandfather's voice. Though she couldn't grasp his words, she understood he was yelling an order. A man answered him, and people were running about in the courtyard.

Had she slept so soundly as to miss the rooster's crowing and also Simha the *shammash's* loud knocking on the shutters at daybreak? Looking around, she saw that Zipporah, too, was still buried under her blankets.

A pungent smell was slowly filling the room, causing Elvina to cough. Her throat was burning. She rushed to the window and lifted the canvas. The courtyard was dark, and yet the sky was lit up with a strange light. It was not the light of a full moon. It looked more like an unnatural, very red dawn, on the opposite side from that on which the sun rose each morning. And in this unnaturally red sky billowed huge black clouds.

Far away, church bells were ringing. Elvina wondered why the bells of the nearby church weren't ringing, but at that moment she heard the cries: "Fire! Fire!"

She heard her father running down the wood stairs, yelling something.

Zipporah jumped out of bed. Miriam rushed into the room coughing and hurriedly wrapping her headscarf around her head. "The church is burning!" she screamed.

All three of them bundled up in their cloaks and hurried down-

143

stairs. They found Solomon ben Isaac ordering every man who came in to run and wake up his neighbors: each man was to take a pail and run to the church in order to help put out the fire.

Yakub ben Yussef, Zakkariya, and their servant were there too, wrapped up in their cloaks, asking Solomon if they could make themselves useful.

"Don't show yourselves! Stay inside the house! People are quick to suspect strangers. You know that as well as I do!" Solomon answered in urgent tones.

Solomon ben Isaac's students rushed into the courtyard, lead by Obadiah, who had already grabbed two pails. Samuel, Yom Tov, and Gauthier were with him. The boys' eyes were puffy, their tunics had been slipped on any which way, their belts knotted haphazardly. Their legs were bare, and some had not even taken the time to put on their sandals. Several were coughing.

Elvina stood next to her father while he distributed pails to the boys. She heard one of them exclaim, "But Master, it's the Sabbath!"

Judah's answer cracked like a whip. "The church is burning! The Sabbath is overridden! It will not be said that the Jews let a church burn down! It's only a small step from there to accusing us of having set it on fire! Enough talk! Run!"

Elvina's heart missed a beat. Ephraim! Could he possibly, in his madness . . . could he have set fire to the church? To avenge his parents? To avenge his community of Mainz, which had been destroyed and plundered? To avenge his beloved synagogue, which had been burned by the Crusaders?

Elvina's throat was so painfully knotted that she could only bend her head when her grandfather ordered her back into the house. The more she thought about it, the more likely it seemed to her that poor miserable Ephraim might very well be responsible for this fire, having been inspired by the evil spirits who were relentlessly tormenting him.

She watched the boys run off, then her father, then her grandfather, who did not run but walked very fast. She watched Precious chasing after Solomon all the way to the entrance of the courtyard and wrapping him up in the warmest cloak she owned, then weeping and wringing her hands as she walked back into her house.

For once, Elvina did not find this habit of her grandmother's to be anything to laugh at. She, too, felt like wringing her hands.

Threatening columns of black smoke rose in the red sky above the roofs. The flames crackled. Elvina shivered. It would have been a thousand times better to run over there with the boys and carry pails of water, to do something, anything, instead of staying home waiting, feeling like a useless fool, and all the while thinking, deep down, that it might have been Ephraim who . . .

Her grandmother grabbed her by the arm. "Follow me, child. We have plenty to do right here. We need to prepare for their return. In what condition will they be, poor things?"

Still hanging on to Elvina, Precious ordered Zipporah to lock up Judah ben Nathan's house. Then, turning to Miriam she said: "Let's all wait in my house! Who knows if some Christians might not get it into their heads to come and seek revenge! At least we will be together!"

"Take me too, please, Mistress Precious, I beg you!"

It was the old beggar. He had crawled into Solomon's courtyard and was exhausted and sobbing with fear.

Precious motioned him into her house. "Come! You will share our fate, whatever it may be!"

Then she closed the window shutter tight and barred the door so that nobody could hear what was happening outside. The Spanish visitors went back up to the room that had been prepared for them. Zakkariya would have much preferred to remain downstairs, but Elvina heard Yakub ben Yussef saying to him, "Come, my son. In the absence of the master of the house, our presence would only be inconvenient and obtrusive for our hostess."

Before going up the stairs, he turned to Miriam. "I hope with all my heart that things will not come to that, but you must know that the three of us are armed and ready to defend the house!"

Elvina couldn't help noticing that Zakkariya was looking at her and smiling, while approving what his father had said. She nodded politely.

What about her? How would she defend poor Ephraim if, as she greatly feared, he had been the one who started the fire?

The first to return were the boys, after the rooster had already crowed.

Chapter

38

Solomon ben Isaac and Judah ben Nathan had remained at the scene of the fire to speak with the priests and the Christian leaders and assure them of the support and assistance of the Jewish community. Then they had gone directly to the synagogue for the morning prayer.

Elvina's grandmother counted the boys: none was missing, thank God! The boys' faces, their hands, their clothes were black with soot and dripping with water. All reeked of smoke. Their eyes were red, all were coughing. A good number of hands and knees were bleeding. Precious, Miriam, Elvina, and the servants ran about, bringing the boys what they needed to wash. They placed compresses on eyes, cleaned and bandaged scraped skin, distributed red poppy syrup to soothe burning throats and a concoction made of dried figs boiled in milk to calm the coughs.

Obadiah and Gauthier sat side by side at the table, both equally filthy, disheveled, and worn out. Elvina brought them washcloths, which she had dipped in chamomile tea. "Apply those to your eyes," she ordered them.

With exactly the same gesture, both pressed the compresses on their burning eyes. Then, since neither could see her, Elvina took a long look at the two of them and, forgetting her own worries for a moment, laughed silently: they were so alike, the dark-haired one and the fair one, the Jewish schoolmaster and the young Christian knight, leaning on their elbows, grunting with exhaustion as well as relief!

According to Samuel the men and boys had formed a chain going from the well to the church in order to pass the buckets full of water in one direction and the empty ones in the other. The wooden statues and the benches had been saved, and also the lower part of the frame, but not the upper part. Yom Tov described how, all of a sudden, there was a loud cry.

"Everyone raised their heads just in time to see the beams and

146

lathes of the roof going up in flames and then the tiles fell into the church, like rain."

Precious let out a horrified scream. "Were people hurt?"

"No, thank God. All were able to escape," Obadiah answered, raising his face out of his compress.

"Thank Heaven!"

At every moment, Precious cast an anxious look toward the courtyard, but, as usual, it was Zipporah who first sighted them. "Master Solomon! Master Judah!"

Solomon ben Isaac's face was gray with fatigue, he was out of breath, but his eyes sparkled. His wife immediately made him settle down in his armchair, then she bustled about, ordering the servants to bring hot wine, humid compresses, bread, eggs that had been boiled before the Sabbath, cheese . . .

Miriam was doing exactly the same for Judah.

Solomon ben Isaac recited the blessing over the wine, then the bread. Then he ate and drank.

"Does anyone know what caused the fire?" Yakub ben Yussef, who had entered the room so discreetly that no one had noticed him, asked the question all had on their lips.

The loud sigh of relief given out simultaneously by Solomon and Judah was his answer even before Solomon spoke in reply. "Yes. Nothing to do with the Jews! The Holy One Blessed be He has willed it that there be no suspicion against us. The fire came from one of the wooden huts built against the side of the church. A drunken man fell asleep and did not watch his fire. He was able to save himself, but all the huts burned."

"They'll still make the Jews pay for the reconstruction of the church. Wait and see," wailed Precious.

Solomon ben Isaac laughed. "You speak the truth, as always, my dear Precious. Let us give thanks to the Almighty that nothing worse has happened to us this year."

"But we are already crumbling under taxes!"

"We are contributing to the prosperity of this good land of Champagne."

All in the room had become silent. "And now, is it the Sabbath again?" asked Yom Tov.

Everyone burst out laughing. Solomon laughed loudest. "Yes, my son, it is the Sabbath. Now go off to the synagogue, all of you, then come back and eat."

The moment has come, thought Elvina. She sat down near Solomon. "I have something important to tell my grandfather in confidence," she began.

Solomon put his hand on her head. "For once, my granddaughter's worries will have to wait. Your old grandfather is exhausted. I don't even have the strength to return to the synagogue. We will speak this afternoon." He looked tenderly at Elvina. "I can see that you are also tired. Why don't you eat, then go and rest a little? It will be well deserved."

Everyone had eaten. Now Zipporah was snoring louder than ever, Judah and Miriam were asleep in their room, and the boys had returned to their dormitory, after having stuffed themselves with eggs, bread, and cheese. Yakub ben Yussef and Zakkariya had gone off to the synagogue.

Elvina got up and walked gingerly down the wooden stairs, hoping the steps wouldn't creak. She wrapped herself in her cloak, carefully lifted the bar from the door, which Miriam had shut tight, and made her escape.

In the courtyard, the old beggar was fast asleep, his head resting on a stone.

The streets still smelled of smoke and were quiet. The shops were closed. The Sabbath now claimed its rights. A few women were chatting on their doorsteps. They were discussing the fire, of course. Several greeted Elvina.

She didn't go directly to Columba's. First she walked to the synagogue, then she went around again through the alley, and finally she walked toward the forge and the blacksmith's shop without meeting anyone.

She had to wait a long time for Ephraim to climb up the ladder and open his trapdoor. He was very pale, there were dark circles under his eyes, and his eyes were feverish. Both lamps burned in the cellar.

No sooner had Elvina set foot on the ground, than Ephraim ran up the steps, locked the trapdoor, and jumped back down. He faced El-vina, but he was agitated and not really looking at her. "I saw the flames. They are burning the city," he said.

"I just came to wish you a good Sabbath," Elvina responded. "The fire does not concern us."

Ephraim did not pay the slightest attention to what she was say-ing. He continued as he had started. "They're surrounding us. But here, with me, you are safe. They won't find us. And if they did find us, I have my knife. I will not let you fall alive into their hands, I promise you."

Elvina tried to quell the fear that was rising in her. "Listen, Ephraim, I'm telling you, this fire is of no concern to us. Today is the Sabbath. The grandfather I have been telling you about is back in Troyes. I want you to come with me to the synagogue."

Ephraim was now looking away from her. "Ephraim," she begged him, "for the past week, you have done everything I wanted you to do. I didn't hurt you or cause you any harm, did I? You know I wish you no harm, don't you?"

"Why would my sister wish me harm?"

"Then come with me to the synagogue!"

"I'm not going anywhere, and neither are you. You're staying here."

Just at that moment, they heard a key click in the lock, and the trapdoor opened: it was Columba. As quick and nimble as a cat, Ephraim leaped up the ladder, grabbed Columba, threw her down, and locked the trapdoor. It happened so fast that all Elvina could do was help Columba get back on her feet. Columba was rubbing one of her knees and crying very loudly. Elvina put her arms around her and held her close. "When he pulled me in, I dropped the key outside. Someone will find it and free us," Columba whispered in her ear. Elvina hugged her once more, then wiped her face dry and smiled at her, marveling at the presence of mind of this tiny and seemingly frail girl.

Ephraim pushed Elvina and Columba to the far end of the cellar and ordered them to sit on the mattress. Then he started walking back and forth. At times he would speak to them gently and kindly, telling them not to be afraid, that he would protect them.

When he was far from them, Columba whispered some explanations into Elvina's ear. "I first came out of the house without my key, because of the Sabbath. But when I saw that the cellar was locked up, I went back to get it, thinking that maybe there was a life to save."

Time went by. It seemed to be getting toward midday because they heard Columba's parents leave the house to go to the synagogue. "Be quiet!" Ephraim commanded the girls. "If you make any kind of sound, I'll kill you. We shall not fall into their hands."

For a moment the girls hoped against hope that Columba's parents would see the key. But no. They walked away. "Isn't your mother going to wonder where you are?" Elvina asked.

"She'll think I've gone to your house. I have spoken to her many times about my new friend Elvina. She is so grateful to you!"

"Where are your brothers?"

"Already at the synagogue, I imagine, with the other boys. And this is the first time my mother has gone to the services since our arrival here."

"Every Jew in town will be there, today, after having been saved from a double danger last night, that of fire and that of wrongful accusation!" Elvina said.

Ephraim was frowning, his eyes more feverish than ever. "They are fools, those who believe they have escaped from danger!"

More time passed. Ephraim took out his mirrors, but he only looked into the mirror of the past. In it he saw his synagogue going up in flames and his grandfather, his parents, and his sisters being killed by the Crusaders. When the girls moved ever so slightly, he threatened them, and once, he even pointed his knife at them.

The two girls held hands to keep up their spirits and their courage. Elvina recited her favorite passages of the week's portion, on this second Sabbath of the month of Iyyar. She spoke of the commandments of the Almighty, who ordered the Jews to leave behind some wheat and some grapes at harvest time so that the poor could come and help themselves, and who ordered them never to insult a deaf person or trip a blind person.

Ephraim advised the girls to lie down and sleep. "You have nothing to fear. I'll be watching over you," he repeated several times, almost tenderly.

Columba did doze off, her head on Elvina's shoulder. Elvina

closed her eyes but did not sleep. The small familiar voice deep inside her, the voice that only she could hear, was moaning and complaining: "For once, now, you're listening to me, obviously you have no choice; you have nothing else to do. Well, girl, you've got yourself into a fine mess, haven't you—and don't say I didn't warn you!" Elvina repressed a little sob. "Mazal, dear Mazal, I can see why you might be extremely angry at your poor, reckless Elvina. But please! Columba also has a *mazal*, of course, so couldn't the two of you put your heads together and think of something? Don't leave us too long in this cellar, guarded by this boy with mad eyes!"

Chapter
39

The synagogue was packed. The stone arches echoed with the sound of prayers and chants. Even the women's section was crowded. Women who had never been seen at the synagogue had come today to give thanks to the Almighty!

Several women whose children had recovered or were well on their way to recovery waved to Miriam and smiled at her in gratitude. The mother of little Toby, now named David, was there, as was Jaquet's mother. Rosa and Flora sat next to Miriam. "Where is Mistress Precious?" they whispered to her.

"She is resting. The night has been a hard one."

"What about your beloved Elvina?"

"I imagine she's keeping her grandmother company."

Judah ben Nathan, Joseph ben Simon, Nathan ben Simon, father of Toby-David, and several other men of the community each read a passage of the week's portion. After each reading, Judah ben Nathan translated the passage into the everyday language so that all would understand. All paid particular attention when Judah ben Nathan recited the special blessing for those who have been saved from danger. And all responded in unison: "He who has shown you every kindness, may He ever deal kindly with you."

The only one not paying attention was Obadiah. He read, when his turn came, then he tried to listen. He tried to focus his attention on the sacred text, but it was in vain. He wondered if he might not be ill. He thought he might feel better if he went out to breathe a little fresh air.

In front of the synagogue, he found Naomi and Rachel. They were squatting on the synagogue steps, looking gloomy. He greeted them with a nod.

"We were sure we'd find Elvina here. She's abandoned us. She has no time for us any more!" they complained. Then, looking up at Obadiah's face, they burst out laughing. "The schoolmaster seems just as disappointed as we are!"

Not bothering to answer, Obadiah stepped back into the synagogue. But almost immediately, something made him come back out again. The twins had walked away and were heading toward the alley. He decided to follow them.

Rachel and Naomi entered Solomon ben Isaac's courtyard. Zipporah was dozing on the bench in the sun.

"Good Sabbath, Zipporah! Is Elvina here?"

"You take her for a giddy scatterbrain like yourselves? Elvina is at the synagogue, of course. Mistress Precious is sleeping. And I am resting, so don't you bother me!"

The twins walked back to the street and cried out in surprise. Obadiah was standing before them!

"Did you hear that? Elvina's not at home! Would you also be looking for her, by any chance?" they teased him.

But the expression on Obadiah's face put a stop to any desire to tease or laugh. They began to feel a little worried.

"Where could she be?" asked Naomi.

"That's what I was about to ask you. Think," said Obadiah. "A little while ago, you told me she had no time for you any more. Who is she spending her time with?"

"Her cousin Fleurdelys!"

"Her cousin Fleurdelys is gone."

"Her handsome young Christian knight, whom she is teaching to read." Rachel was immediately sorry she had spoken those words. "Forgive me, Obadiah, I'm being mean."

Obadiah shrugged his shoulders. "She would not be teaching him to read on a Sabbath, when everybody is at the synagogue giving thanks to the Almighty. Think of something else."

"Columba!" the twins cried. Then, "Columba isn't at the synagogue either!"

"Who is Columba?"

"The German girl."

"Godolias's sister?"

"Yes. Columba has all the qualities we don't have. She's much more learned than we are and . . ."

Obadiah cut them short. "Where does she live?"

"You know where she lives. Near Dieulesault's forge, you know, in the house that burned last year. Come! We'll take you there!"

When Ephraim heard the key turning in the lock, he jumped to his feet and ran to the ladder. The girls got up too.

The trapdoor opened. Ephraim stood ready, teeth clenched, knife in hand.

"Obadiah, be careful! He is mad! He has a knife!" Elvina screamed out as she recognized the schoolmaster.

Obadiah climbed down the ladder without taking his eyes off Ephraim. When he started speaking, he spoke very softly in the calm, self-assured voice of a schoolmaster accustomed to controlling his students.

"Good Sabbath! My name is Obadiah. I'm a friend. I do not wish you any harm. What is your name?"

"His name is Ephraim," Elvina answered.

Obadiah and Ephraim stood face to face. Obadiah was taller, but Ephraim was strong and armed. Obadiah continued to speak in the same even tone of voice. "It is the Sabbath, today, Ephraim. These two girls must go to the synagogue. You and I could escort them. We would be doing a good deed."

Ephraim unclenched his teeth just enough to declare, "They're not going anywhere."

Elvina and Columba clung to each other, barely breathing. Obadiah stretched out his hand toward them, motioning them to walk forward. They took a step.

Already Ephraim was brandishing his knife. "I'll sacrifice my sister rather than let her fall into their hands."

Never raising his voice, Obadiah answered Ephraim. "I understand you, and I feel the same way. But the moment has not come for that. Meanwhile, why don't you hide your knife under your mattress, or, if you want, you can trust me with it."

The girls let out a cry. They saw Ephraim fall on Obadiah, his knife raised to strike. They saw the blade flash. Obadiah's sleeve began to turn red.

The struggle did not last long. Obadiah disarmed Ephraim, who cowered up against the wall. Obadiah slid the knife under the straw mattress. When he spoke, he spoke very calmly, as if his left arm were not covered with blood.

"Ephraim, your duty was to protect these two girls, and you have done your duty. You are a worthy son of Israel and in a short while our master Solomon ben Isaac will thank you himself. Up to now, you were right to keep the girls in the cellar, but now several people know of this hiding place. It would be a good thing if you—if we—took them somewhere else, to a place where we can continue to protect them."

Ephraim's eyes were staring out in the distance, gazing at something only he was able to see.

After a brief silence, Obadiah spoke again. "We should start without further delay. I know the way. There is nothing to fear."

Ephraim walked toward his pile of clothes, grabbed his two mirrors and held them tightly against his chest. "Rabbi Simeon bar Isaac had several of them. I only have two. I'm taking them with me."

Elvina held her breath. Would Obadiah permit Ephraim to go out on the streets carrying his mirrors on the Sabbath? She said, in a small voice, "Ephraim sees the past in one of his mirrors. I tried to show him the future in the other mirror. I'm the one who gave it to him."

Obadiah looked at Ephraim for a long while. Elvina was looking at Obadiah. She could read in his eyes the same pity that she herself had been feeling, these past few days, for the skinny boy gone mad with grief.

Very gently, Obadiah said, "Take your mirrors."

The voice that spoke these words exactly resembled the kind, compassionate voice of Solomon ben Isaac. And now, Elvina began to cry. She wasn't quite sure why she was crying. Fatigue and relief, yes, but also from a vague sadness that was not really sadness, and which in the end, as she wiped her cheeks with her sleeve, caused her to smile at Obadiah as she had never smiled at anyone before.

Chapter

40

Out on the street, Rachel and Naomi waited impatiently. As soon as they saw Elvina climbing out of the trapdoor they rushed up to her and hugged her. "Elvina, poor Elvina, you're pale, you're dirty, your eyes are red! Were you locked up?"

Elvina took a few deep breaths. Never had air tasted so delicious!

"All is well, thank God! But now, run off, I beg you! We are going to take an unhappy and terrified boy over to my grandfather's house. If he sees a lot of people on the street, he will be frightened and escape from us."

"You'll tell us everything later?"

"Yes, I promise. You can inform your aunt Flora that her mirror has been found. We'll return it to her, but not right now. I'll explain it all."

Obadiah and Elvina walked on either side of Ephraim. Ephraim walked stiffly, looking straight ahead of him, without turning his head left or right. He was hugging his mirrors but no one could see them because Elvina had wrapped her own cloak around the boy. Columba walked next to Elvina, holding her hand. From time to time, Obadiah said a few words of encouragement to Ephraim, telling him they would be perfectly safe in the new place to which he was leading them.

They avoided walking by the synagogue so as not to meet those coming out, and they reached Solomon ben Isaac's courtyard without running into any difficulty. As they entered Solomon's house, Elvina kissed her grandmother and whispered some quick explanations into her ear.

Ephraim went straight to the farthest, darkest corner of the room and sat down on the ground. Elvina brought a pitcher of wine and cups, then she sat down next to him. Columba and Obadiah did the same.

At last they heard steps in the courtyard. Ephraim frowned and looked worried, but Obadiah placed a reassuring hand on his shoulder as Solomon ben Isaac walked into the room with quick steps. Elvina and Obadiah stood up. Elvina announced, "We've brought Ephraim ben Isaac ben Judah ben Meshullam."

Then all witnessed an extraordinary thing: Solomon's features lit up. He was gazing on Ephraim with a joy such as his family had almost never seen on his face. "Blessed be the Almighty who grants that I should see with my own eyes, alive and in my house, the grandson of my friend Kalonymos ben Meshullam HaParnas, leader of the community of Mainz! Kalonymos ben Meshullam was your mother's father, was he not, my son?"

Ephraim seemed fascinated. His eyes were riveted on Solomon's face and his own face had brightened up a little. But he did not stand up, did not walk toward Solomon, did not bow to him, did not move from his place on the ground. He just answered, "Yes."

Solomon went to Ephraim, lifted him up, and held him close. He took Ephraim's face between his two hands, looked deeply into his eyes, and his joy turned into a great sadness. Solomon put his arms around the boy. The silver hair and beard mixed with the long dark mane.

Solomon ben Isaac wept on Ephraim's shoulder and Ephraim did not try to push him away or escape. Then Solomon regained his self-control. He moved back a little, without letting go of the boy, and spoke to him with a great tenderness. "May you be blessed, Ephraim ben Isaac, son and grandson of martyrs! Your grandfather was the companion of my youth; we studied together at the feet of the same masters. But he, Kalonymos ben Meshullam, your grandfather, is truly great for all eternity. He protects us and will protect generations to come because his death was the death of the righteous."

He kissed and hugged Ephraim again and asked him, "What are you holding, my son?"`

"My mirrors."

"Your mirrors?"

"Our master Simeon bar Isaac the Great of Mainz owned several of them."

Solomon was intently observing Ephraim. "I see," he said.

Elvina stood close to Ephraim. "When I found Ephraim, he only had the mirror of the past. I'm the one who gave him the second mirror. I was hoping to help him see the future," she explained, then her voice quivered a little as she added, "I failed."

Ephraim now said, "My sister Bona refuses to understand that our grandfather is dead."

Solomon's eyes went from Elvina, who was exhausted and red-eyed, to Columba, whom he had never seen before, to Obadiah, who had left the synagogue long before the end of the service. He saw the blood on Obadiah's sleeve. Once again he put his arms around Ephraim's shoulders and said, "If you wish, my son, we shall look together into the mirror of the past."

In the large room now filled with the oblique and yellow rays of the late afternoon sun, Precious examined Obadiah's arm. She decided not to wait until the end of the Sabbath to clean the wound with wine. Later on, she would apply a compress with egg whites to make it heal properly. Meanwhile, she served all of them bowls filled with her delicious Sabbath stew. Ephraim, seated next to Obadiah, ate a few mouthfuls of it.

Then Solomon took Ephraim with him into his study, which was next to the big room. Soon they heard Ephraim chanting. But he was not chanting the sacred text.

"He's reading from the mirror of the past," explained Elvina.

Then they heard Solomon's serious, firm voice, as if he were reciting, slowly, insisting on each word. "I see the city of Mainz and her streets that go down to the river. I see the boy Ephraim walking with his grandfather along the frozen river. They are admiring the ships trapped in the ice. Ephraim accompanies his grandfather on his visits to the poor of the community. He rejoices at the love and respect everyone shows his grandfather. Now I see them in the synagogue. I see Ephraim standing right next to his grandfather, warm and safe inside his grandfather's cloak . . ."

Ephraim interrupted him. "The flames are rising, the Torah scrolls are being trampled and burned . . ."

"Look, my son, look again. We see the day Ephraim is called to the Torah for the first time. He is standing between his father, Isaac ben Judah, and his grandfather, Kalonymos ben Meshullam. Both are proud, so proud of young Ephraim, and his mother and sisters are weeping with joy as they hear him read for the first time in the synagogue of Mainz."

Again Ephraim interrupted him, angrily this time. "Ephraim's grandfather is sitting in the bishop's courtyard. His prayer shawl is soaked in blood. Kalonymos ben Meshullam is dead . . ."

And once more, Solomon replied with infinite patience, "I see Kalonymos ben Meshullam reading the Talmud with Ephraim. His eyes are shining with joy as he listens to his grandson reading and reciting. Nothing in the world is more important to him than that. Kalonymos ben Meshullam asks, 'And how does my erudite study companion explain this passage?' He smiles at his grandson, a mischievous smile, and then he argues, waving his hand in a manner that belongs only to him . . ."

Ephraim's voice was a little hoarse now. "My grandfather always waves his hand in this way when he argues."

Some time later, Solomon walked out alone from his study and came to sit at the table next to Elvina.

"Young Ephraim has fallen asleep, rolled up under your cloak."

Elvina told her grandfather everything. About the cellar, the stolen margins, the knife. The week she spent trying to heal Ephraim. The madder plants. The egg. The mirrors, one of which had been stolen from Flora.

"Maybe I acted wrongly," she concluded. "I wanted to protect him against . . . against . . . well . . . until my grandfather's return from Châlons. There were the sick children and all these people who were so angry . . ."

Solomon placed his hand on her head. He was smiling. "No one can ever accuse my granddaughter of being overly careful, or of lacking in generosity. What does Obadiah ben Moyses think?"

Glancing around, Elvina saw Obadiah sitting on the bench, leaning against the wall. She realized he hadn't lost a single word of what she was saying. In his wide open, intensely focused eyes, she read neither the fatigue of a night spent fighting the fire, nor the pain his wound was most certainly causing him. What she read in Obadiah's eyes was . . . yes, admiration, an admiration he made no effort to conceal as he answered, in his usual even tone of voice, "Our master speaks the truth."

"When I think of everything that could have happened!" Precious moaned.

"But didn't happen, my dear Precious!" Solomon was still smiling.

Then, to Elvina, he said, "Your idea of giving Ephraim the mirror of the future was an excellent one, but he is not yet ready to look at the future. For now, I shall examine with him the mirror of the past. We shall cure him. And until he is cured, we will have to watch him day and night. We don't want any more slaughtered animals."

While Elvina had been telling her story, the day had been moving toward twilight. Darkness was slowly settling in the big room. Solomon now turned to Columba. "You are Ephraim's cousin?"

"His father, Isaac ben Judah, was my mother's brother," Columba answered in a very small and terrified voice.

"Be most welcome in our house. But it is getting late. A servant will escort you home. You will tell your parents that Solomon ben Isaac is inviting your entire family to join us for the Sabbath dinner next week. I have every reason to hope that we shall be able, then, to offer our thanks to the Almighty. I have been assured that the children are all well on their way to recovery and that there are no new cases of the fever."

These last words were addressed to Precious, whose old wrinkled face lit up for a brief moment, as she replied with a worried smile, but nevertheless a smile, "Not one, thank God, not a single new case this week!"

A cry came from the courtyard. It was Yom Tov yelling, "*Havdalah*! *Havdalah*! Three medium-sized stars are visible in the sky! And I saw the rooster jump down from his perch and walk back into the chicken house with his hens . . ."

He was still speaking breathlessly as he ran in. "I hear Elvina has been locked up in a cellar, and my master Obadiah ben Moyses is horribly wounded, and there is a strange boy who . . ."

Solomon silenced him with a gesture of his hand. "Calm yourself, my son. Your master is in good health. Greet him with the respect you owe him."

Just behind Yom Tov, Gauthier and Samuel entered the room. Samuel glared at Elvina. "There's always something interesting happening to my cousin!" he said.

Solomon bowed slightly in Gauthier's direction. "The young knight has come to visit us?"

Samuel spoke for Gauthier. "Gauthier has come to beg my grandfather to permit him to attend his class tomorrow morning before he has to leave. He has been studying very hard all week long to be able to understand, if only a few words."

Solomon nodded. A glimmer of a smile crossed his lips, as he replied, "Our young knight is not easily discouraged from his study program, I see. Permission is granted. But the moment has come to recite *Havdalah*. And here come Judah ben Nathan and my daughter Miriam."

Miriam ran straight up to Elvina and anxiously patted her forehead and her cheeks. "Are you feeling well, child? You seem tired! Didn't you rest today?"

Solomon motioned her to be quiet. He asked Samuel to bring the fancy chiseled silver spice box and to fill it with fragrant spices. Judah had already placed the wine and the lamp on the table.

Solomon ben Isaac blessed the wine and the spices, drank the wine, and then burned the spices so that their fragrance would spread all around the house, that all might breathe it as a consolation for the departure of the Sabbath.

Suddenly out of the darkness walked Ephraim, still wrapped in Elvina's cloak. He walked toward the table. His face was expressionless, but his eyes searched around until he saw Obadiah, then, without hesitation, he went and stood next to him. His eyes came to rest upon Solomon's face, glowing in the light of the lamp Judah had just lit. Judah blessed the light, and everyone, Solomon ben Isaac, Judah ben Nathan, Precious and Miriam, Obadiah, Samuel and Yom Tov, Elvina and old Zipporah, and Gauthier, who carefully imitated Samuel, all looked at the flame through their fingers and fingernails.

Elvina noticed that even Ephraim finally stretched his fingers toward the dancing flame. She saw, right next to Ephraim's bony fingers, Obadiah's hands, his large, strong, reassuring hands, which she had so often watched him place on the boys' heads in his classroom. She saw that Obadiah was looking straight at her, and that he was smiling.

She returned his gaze without averting her eyes because the best way to bless the light is by gazing upon the faces of those one loves.

She thought, you can't possibly have any objection to that, can you, Mazal? Dearest Mazal!

Glossary

afikoman: A piece of matzah that is hidden by the leader at the Passover (Pesach) meal, and which must be found at the end, to be eaten as "dessert."

haroset: A thick mixture of red wine, chopped apples, nuts, dates, figs, and spices, such as ginger and cinnamon; it symbolizes the mortar the Hebrews used when they were slaves in Egypt and made bricks for the pharaohs.

Havdalah: The ritual marking the end of the Sabbath.

matzot (singular: matzah): Cakes of unleavened bread eaten during the Passover (Pesach) festival. The *matzot* are a symbol of freedom because God took the Hebrews out of Egypt so quickly that their dough did not have time to rise. But *matzot* also represent the bread of affliction, the kind of bread the Hebrews ate in Egypt when they were slaves.

mazal: A guardian angel. According to Jewish belief, every human has a *mazal* to plead his or her cause in heaven. In the Talmud and Midrash, *mazal* also means a constellation of the zodiac, and destiny. It is associated with intelligence (the ability to avoid danger) and with luck, as in "*mazel tov*," which means "good luck."

mazzikim (singular: *mazzik*): Evil spirits. Certain legends say that *mazzikim* are souls of the wicked transformed into demons as punishment. They have several things in common with angels: they have wings and fly from one end of the earth to the other, they can see the future, and of course they are invisible.

mezuzot (singular: mezuzah): Strips of parchment on which the two first paragraphs of the Shema have been copied by hand. They are then rolled and placed in small boxes made of wood, metal, or other material, and hung on the right side of doors.

Mishnah: A collection of traditional laws and decisions, called the Oral Law, set down in writing in Hebrew at the end of the second century CE (common era). The Talmud, written by later generations of rabbis, contains commentary on and discussion of the Mishnah.

Midrash: Tales and legends of the rabbis that comment on the Torah and other books of the Bible. There are many different collections of them.

parashah: The Torah is divided into fifty-four parts, each of which is called a parashah. Each Saturday in the synagogue the parashah of the week is read.

Passover (Hebrew: Pesach): A festival commemorating the liberation of the Hebrews, who were enslaved by the pharaohs, and their flight from Egypt. Under the leadership of Moses, the Hebrews were guided through the Sinai Desert for forty years as they made their way to the Promised Land.

responsum (plural: responsa): A written decision from a rabbinic authority in response to a submitted question or problem.

Sabbath: The seventh day of the week, a day of rest in Jewish households. The Sabbath begins at sundown on Friday evening and lasts until nightfall on Saturday. It is a day of joy; the house must be cleaned and food prepared in advance, so the whole day may be given over to rest, prayer or study, conversations with friends, or walks. The Sabbath ends with *Havdalah,* a ceremony marking the separation between the Sabbath and everyday life. Wine, perfume, and light receive a special blessing.

Talmud: The interpretation and elaboration of the Mishnah, also called the Oral Law, by rabbis who discuss its meaning. The Talmud was written in Hebrew and Aramaic in Palestine and Babylon between the third and fifth centuries CE (common era).

Temple: The First Temple was constructed by King Solomon in Jerusalem in the tenth century BCE (before the common era). The Ark was kept in a part of the Temple called the Holy of Holies, a place where only the High Priest was allowed to enter and only on the Day of Atonement. The First Temple was destroyed in 586 BCE. The Second Temple was built in 516 BCE and was destroyed by the Romans in 70 CE. One wall of the Second Temple still remains, and it is known today as the Western Wall or Wailing Wall.

Torah: The root of this word means "to teach." The Torah is the scroll that contains the Five Books of Moses, which are Genesis, Exodus, Leviticus, Numbers, and Deuteronomy.